UNDERHAND

orca sports

UNDERHAND

M.J. McISAAC

ORCA BOOK PUBLISHERS

Library and Archives Canada Cataloguing in Publication

McIsaac, M. J., 1986-, author
Underhand / M.J. McIsaac.
(Orca sports)

Issued in print and electronic formats.
ISBN 978-1-4598-0416-6 (pbk.).--978-1-4598-0758-7 (bound)
ISBN 978-1-4598-0417-3 (pdf).--ISBN 978-1-4598-0418-0 (epub)

I. Title. II. Series: Orca sports
PS8625.I85U64 2014 jC813'.6 C2013-906849-X
C2013-906850-3

First published in the United States, 2014
Library of Congress Control Number: 2013952685

Summary: Nick is determined to clear his brother's name when a vicious rumor jeopardizes Markus's lacrosse scholarship.

Orca Book Publishers is dedicated to preserving the environment and has printed this book on Forest Stewardship Council® certified paper.

Orca Book Publishers gratefully acknowledges the support for its publishing programs provided by the following agencies: the Government of Canada through the Canada Book Fund and the Canada Council for the Arts, and the Province of British Columbia through the BC Arts Council and the Book Publishing Tax Credit.

Cover photography by Corbis Images
Author photo by Crystal Jones

ORCA BOOK PUBLISHERS
PO Box 5626, Stn. B
Victoria, BC Canada
V8R 6S4

ORCA BOOK PUBLISHERS
PO Box 468
Custer, WA USA
98240-0468

www.orcabook.com
Printed and bound in Canada.

17 16 15 14 • 4 3 2 1

For my brothers—Graeme, Will and Alex—
who know about this stuff.

chapter one

Looking at the world from behind a cage does something to the brain. You see a tiger pacing back and forth and people say he's bored. I don't know about that. I think he's probably just fired up. Ready to break out and take no prisoners. That's how it is for me anyway, when I put on that helmet and see the world from behind those bars.

My cheeks feel like they're the surface of the sun. I can feel the sweat beneath my pads, dripping down my back. I'm soaked.

My muscles are burning, and I push my feet as fast as they can go. My limbs feel like rubber.

The ball is mine, safely nestled in the pocket of my stick while I barrel for the net. There's a thumping behind me, the steady pounding of the left creaseman coming to stop me.

"Look who you got, Nick!" Coach is screaming from the bench.

Out of the corner of my eye, I see my teammate tearing up the left side. That's who I got. But I don't need him. Coach'll see–*I've* got this.

And then he's hitting me, the left crease. My right shoulder tenses as he swats at my stick with his.

"Nick!" my teammate screams. "Over here!"

I ignore him. The net is calling my name.

I drop my stick and rip an underhand shot, bottom right–their goalie can't block it. And then a body, the left crease, cross-checks me on my right side and I'm knocked off my feet.

The whistle blows. Practice is over.

I lie there, staring at the arena's ceiling. Banners with our team's name on them, *Maplehurst Vikings*, hang down from the rafters. Coach is gonna kill me. My lungs swell until they're ready to burst. I try to ignore the tingling where my shoulder bit the concrete.

"Nick!" My teammate stands over me and takes off his helmet. I see the shaved-head silhouette of Markus, my brother. A bead of sweat from the end of his nose drops through my face mask, and I spit. "I was wide open. What the hell, man?"

He was. I spit again.

"Markus!" shouts Coach Preston from the bench. "Get changed, then come see me."

I'm a little relieved Coach didn't ask for me. Then again, he's said plenty to me today already. I guess he's finally given up.

Markus sighs and wipes his nose on the back of his sleeve. He nudges me with his foot. "Wait for me by the car."

When I don't say anything, he shakes his head and follows the rest of the Vikings to the change room.

I still lie there on the floor, staring up at the ceiling.

chapter two

There's this crusty smell that seeps out of my lacrosse bag. It's always strongest after practice. Like hot dogs that have been left out in the sun for a long time. And lemons, from whatever spray my mom tries to hose it down with. Sunbaked hot dogs and lemons. That's the after-practice stink.

I sit on one of those cement things, the kind you park your car against. Maybe I should open up my bag, air it out a little.

My nose scrunches. I don't really want to have to sit here and smell it though.

"You look glum, Nickadoo." It's Lindy Hilner. I know it even before I turn around to see her rolling up in her blue Acura. She's at all our games, always volunteers to be timekeeper. Even though she's been doing it forever, she hardly ever talks to me. But when she does, she calls me Nickadoo. She's called me that since I was in third grade and she was in fourth with Markus. I'm in tenth now, and you'd think I wouldn't like it. But since she lost her braces and stopped wearing overalls, it's hard not to like.

"What?" I say, noticing the pink tank top she's wearing.

"You look down."

"Rough practice," I tell her. That's an understatement. Practice was more than rough.. With provincials coming up and Maplehurst hosting this year, the town's expecting a lot from us. The Vikings have been provincial champs for nine years in a row, and this year's supposed to be ten.

Coach has been feeling the pressure, getting on my case every minute. I wouldn't mind if it was because I was messing up a lot, or because I was being lazy. But that isn't his problem. The problem Coach has with me is always the same problem. The problem is, I'm not Markus.

"What are you doing?" I ask Lindy, changing the subject.

"Driving." She shrugs.

Obviously. I laugh, but she doesn't say anything more. Is it my turn to say something? She smiles and waits. I guess it is my turn. Two perfect dimples mark either side of her white smile. All I can think of saying is how much I like them.

Lindy tilts her head and stares at the arena doors behind me. Her brow furrows. "Do you need a ride?"

No.

"Yeah!" I blurt out. I don't need a ride. I drove here with Markus. I'm supposed to drive home with Markus. He's got the keys to our van, but he's taking forever. And a chance for one-on-one face time with Lindy

Hilner doesn't come along much for a guy like me.

I hoist my bag over my shoulder and hurry over to the passenger door. The hot dog-lemon stink wafts up to my nose. The last thing I want is to funk up Lindy Hilner's car.

"Pop the trunk," I say.

"What?"

"My bag."

She points her thumb at the back seat. "Just throw it in the back."

I look at Lindy Hilner's pristine back seat. There's a row of small stuffed toys lining the rear window. It's all going to smell like hot dogs and lemons. If I keep the window down, she might not notice. It's either that or beg her to open the trunk, and then she'll think I'm hiding a body or something. I decide to take my chances with the window and chuck the bag in the back.

I plop down in the front beside Lindy and am immediately hit by cinnamon and flowers. Trendy Femme. She's worn it every day since eighth grade. She keeps a bottle in her locker.

She sits there smiling at me and I smile back.

Silence.

She turns away, staring out her window. Is it my turn to talk again?

"Uh, thanks so much for this," I say. "Would've been rough to walk it."

"No worries!" She's not even looking at me. She's facing the arena. I don't know why we're not moving. "How much longer is your brother going to be?"

And there it is. The reason we're not moving. Markus. I should have known that's why she offered me a ride. She never talks to me at our games, but as soon as her clock duties are over, she's right there talking to Markus.

"He's not coming," I say. That's not really true. He could be walking out those arena doors any second. He's been in there with Coach for a good twenty minutes. They have to be almost done.

Lindy stares at me, blinking those big honey-brown eyes.

"He wasn't feeling well," I lie again before I can stop myself. "Got sick before practice, went home."

"Oh." She tilts her head. "He didn't seem sick in class."

"Yeah," I say. "So he's gone. He's not coming."

I feel bad for lying. But Markus has the keys for the van–it's not like I'm leaving him stranded.

"Okay," she says, turning the key. The radio explodes with some Top 40 tune that sounds the way her perfume smells. She shouts something over the music.

"Huh?"

"I said, do you think he'll be at school tomorrow?"

I shrug. I know he will be, but I don't like that she cares.

We fly down Devon Road at what I doubt is the legal speed. The wind smacking my face cools the sweat on my forehead and neck. I notice my hair in the side mirror, a shaggy brown mess of curls. I wish I had a hat.

"Well, if he's not," Lindy shouts, "tell him I can pick up his homework. We do that, me and Markus. You know, if one of us misses something in class."

I try not to raise an eyebrow. Lindy and Markus have drama class together. How much homework can there be?

"That's nice of you," is all I manage.

She grins. "I do what I can."

She watches me out of the corner of her eye. My turn again, I guess.

"I'll tell him," I say. "And you know, if you ever need me to bring you stuff, homework or whatever, I can–"

She starts to sing along to the music before I can finish. She shrugs her shoulders and bobs her head to the heavy bass. I try not to laugh. She sings way off-key, but she's cute when she dances. I recognize the song–it's the theme to that new movie *Fire Heart*. It's playing at the Galaxy Screens, and I wonder if she's seen it yet. I have–it was awful. But if Lindy hasn't, I'd probably see it again.

She reaches over and hits the power button on the stereo. "I'm sorry, Nickadoo," she laughs, "but that bag smells so foul."

My cheeks heat up again.

"That's nothing," I say. "You should smell Markus's." The words just fall out of my mouth.

"It can't be worse than that."

"Trust me, it's worse. Like a million old socks and a dead cat."

She laughs. "Sick."

I laugh too. I've laughed a lot in this car, and we haven't said anything that funny. I bite the inside of my cheek. Maybe I've laughed too much.

Lindy turns the music back on and cranks the volume. She doesn't say anything else until we're in my driveway.

"Thanks for the ride!" I say and hurry to get my bag.

"Sure, no problem. Tell Markus I hope he feels better!"

There's a grinding, rattling noise coming from down the street. There's only one thing that sounds like that. Our van. Markus.

"Sure, I will!" I slam Lindy's door and wave goodbye, hoping she takes off before she sees him.

Too late.

"Nick!" Markus honks at us, his arm hanging out the window. "What the hell? You left!"

Lindy gets out of her car and waves at my brother. I'm busted. Having no better idea of what to do, I run inside the house, slamming the door behind me.

Standing in our dark front hall, my cheeks feel like they're a million degrees, and I hold my breath. Lindy's out there, talking to my brother, finding out I'm nothing but a liar.

chapter three

Lindy Hilner and my brother have been standing in the driveway for ten minutes when she finally decides to leave. I take another swig of orange juice and, through the kitchen window, watch her climb into her blue Acura.

What's got Lindy Hilner thinking Markus is such a big deal anyway? Last year's tournament in Guelph might have done it. Markus had a broken wrist for the final two games, but he played anyway.

And won it for us. Lindy was there, running the clock. He never said anything about his wrist, not until I noticed the swelling. When I pointed it out and we got word that it was a fracture, Coach Preston was more than impressed. So was the team. And apparently, so was Lindy Hilner. Markus Carver, team hero, lacrosse legend.

I hear Mom thumping down the stairs. “Markus? How was practice?”

She bursts into the kitchen and her eyes bulge when she sees me holding the orange-juice carton. “Nicholas! Are you drinking out of the carton again?”

I shake my head and swallow the juice in my cheeks. I reach for a glass to really sell the lie.

“Where’s your brother?”

“He’s coming,” I say. He sure is. I can see him coming up the front path. I’ve got about ten seconds to disappear to the bathroom before he confronts me about Lindy. I can’t go to my room. I share it with Markus. The only real place to be alone in this house is the john.

The door slams and there's a thud as he drops his lacrosse bag. Five seconds.

I rush by Mom and nearly spill my juice. I sprint full tilt for the stairs and *boom!*

My juice goes flying out of my hand as Markus slams me against the banister. He pushes his lacrosse stick hard against my chest. I'm pinned–and covered in OJ.

"Boys!" Mom barks. "Not in the house!"

I struggle against him, but Markus is stronger. He's always been stronger. I wait for him to yell at me, but he doesn't. There's a smirk on his face.

"Look at this, Nick," he says. "I guess I'm feeling better."

I push with all my might and he lets me go.

He laughs. "You said I was sick?"

I say nothing and start to head upstairs. I don't need him making me feel more embarrassed than I already do.

"Relax, Nick," he says. "I told her I was."

I stop a couple of steps up and look at him. "Was what?"

He stands there in the middle of the front hall, grinning. "Sick. I told Lindy I had a stomachache and left practice to get some Tums."

My stress melts away instantly. Lindy doesn't know I lied.

"Wanted to get her alooooone?" he says, puckering his lips.

"Shut up."

"Who?" asks Mom, peeking out from the kitchen. "Who is he getting alone?"

"No one," I say.

"No one," agrees Markus.

Mom isn't that interested anyway. She throws a dishtowel at Markus. "Why are you so late? I was expecting you a half hour ago."

Markus kicks off his sandals and starts to sop up the spilled juice. "Had to talk to Coach."

"About what? Provincials?" she says.

Markus sighs and stops what he's doing. He drops his head and bites his lip. No, not provincials. It must be big.

"He wanted me to meet this guy from Philston Weiks."

"The private school?" says Mom.

He nods. "Home of the Hurricanes. I met the coach."

My juice-soaked shirt feels heavy on my skin, and I lean against the banister. We've played the Hurricanes a few times. Once, maybe twice a year just for fun. We're in different leagues. We play for the city and they play for the Philston Weiks Academy. They travel around the country and a lot of the States. We don't.

"What did he want?" asks Mom. She's grinning from ear to ear, rubbing her hands like she already knows what he's going to say.

"He wants me to play for the Hurricanes," he says. "Full scholarship."

Mom lets out a shriek, and I wince. The sound is like a drill in my ears. She grabs Markus in a hug.

Markus on the Hurricanes? Their coach came to our practice just to ask for Markus?

"Just you?" I ask. "He didn't ask about anybody else?"

Markus doesn't hear me. He's too busy with Mom, who's holding his head in her hands. "Oh, this is so exciting!"

Markus laughs as she hugs him again.

"I was going to make salmon, but I think this is a pizza occasion, don't you?" Smiling, Mom reaches out and grabs my hand that's resting on the banister.

"So," I say, "the Hurricanes' coach was just asking about you?"

Markus says nothing, just sniffs, and Mom's smile goes down a little. She gives my hand a squeeze. "You boys go change, then come down and tell me what you want on your pizzas!"

I nod. Markus's sniff was enough. Just him. No one else.

Mom heads back to the kitchen and Markus disappears to the bathroom, leaving me alone on the stairs. A full scholarship to Philston Weiks, just for Markus.

Just for Markus, and no one else.

chapter four

I didn't go downstairs for pizza. I said I wasn't hungry. My stomach grumbles as I run my pencil along the staples in my notebook. I'm starving, but I don't want to go downstairs. Not yet. Not until Mom and Dad are done raving about Markus's scholarship to Philston Weiks Academy.

I stare at my notebook. I've been staring at the same math problem for over an hour. None of this homework is getting done. With a sigh, I swing around in my chair and lift my feet onto my bed. It's made. Markus's isn't. His bed is a mess, with clothes scattered across his jumbled covers.

It's not that I don't think he deserves to go to Philston Weiks. He does. Markus is a great player–a right shot, like me. It's just that everything seems to happen for Markus. Everything gets served to him on a platter. Even in lacrosse. He's just the triggerman. We'll see how well he does at Philston Weiks when he doesn't have me doing all the work and setting him up for easy goals.

My elbow bumps a textbook sitting at the edge of my desk. It topples to the floor, taking the slushie cup that was sitting on top with it. Melted red slush spills onto the carpet, and I growl. Markus loves cherry slushies. I grab the sweatpants he left sitting on the edge of his bed and start sopping it up.

I hate slushies.

There's a *ding*. It's coming from Markus's computer. I look up from my mess and see an instant message blinking on his monitor. I can just make out the shape of the name–Linds.

Lindy Hilner.

I abandon the mess–it was Markus's slushie anyway–and grab the mouse. What's she messaging Markus for?

I click on her name.

How are you feeling?

I bite the inside of my cheek. I didn't even know he had Lindy in his contacts. I don't.

My fingers flex in front of the keyboard. Markus's keyboard.

F-i-n-e. I type the word quickly and hit Enter without thinking.

Good. That means you can keep your promise!

What promise? Before I know it, I'm typing it out and pressing Enter again.

Freezo's Palace! You said you'd take me tomorrow.

I pull my hands back from the keys. Markus is taking Lindy Hilner out for ice cream. Lindy Hilner wants to go out for ice cream with Markus. The hangnail on my thumb starts to throb, and I chew on it.

I don't know why he'd ask her out. She's not even his type. Markus likes the artsy girls. Musical theater in particular. His last two girlfriends were singing and dancing in our school's terribly PG version of *Chicago*. Lindy can't sing, not even a little.

Can't. My fingers fly across the keys. **I have a game tomorrow.**

That's not a lie. We do have a game. Against the Oak Ridge Timber Wolves.

I know that, dummy, I'm timekeeper. ;)

I never figured Lindy for an emoticon user. I refuse to use them. I think they're stupid and I don't really understand the point. Like right now. What does a winky face have to do with anything? My buddy Kevin once told me that's how girls flirt. My teeth grind when I realize he might be right.

You said you'd take me after. Is that not happening now?

I stare at the words on the screen. **Is that not happening now?**

It *is* happening. Markus is going to take Lindy Hilner out for ice cream after our game. I'll be going home with my mom.

Markus will be climbing into Lindy's blue Acura. That's what's happening. I can't help but wonder if it would be different if he were a Philston Weiks kid. Part of me wishes he'd gone sooner. Then ice cream with Lindy Hilner would not be happening.

She messages him again, just four question marks in a row. I close the box.

Maybe this Philston Weiks thing isn't such a bad idea. If Markus is gone, Coach won't get on my case so much. If Markus is gone, I'll be scoring more. If Markus is gone, he won't have drama class with Lindy Hilner.

There's a growl in my gut. I can't hide out up here anymore.

I click the power button on the monitor and decide to grab what's left of the pizza.

If Markus is gone, things will be better.

chapter five

Muffled bass thumps through the hallway from the change room for Pad 4 at Maplehurst Arena. Just from the rhythm I can tell exactly what song it is. "Rock Monster" by Pound Sound. Kevin's favorite song. "To pump us up," he always says. After hearing it before every game for the last year, I can already feel my heart working a little harder.

Markus shakes his head as we walk toward the change room. "Gotta talk to that idiot about getting a new song."

"It's growing on me," I admit.

We reach the door and I can hear the team on the other side, laughing and shouting. Markus reaches out to push the door open, but I stop him.

"What are you gonna tell the guys?" I ask.

"'Bout what?"

About what. "Uh, about Philston Weiks?"

His jaw tightens, and he grinds his teeth for a second before he says, "Nothing."

"Nothing?!"

"What? It's not official or anything. What's to tell?"

Not official? They offered him a scholarship–how much more official can it get? All that's left to do is say yes.

I grab him by the arm. "Wait, are you thinking of not going?"

Markus looks at my hand on his arm. I realize my grip is probably tighter than it needs to be. I let go. "Are you thinking of not taking the scholarship?"

Markus just shrugs.

"Why not?!"

My voice gets away from me, and the question echoes down the hall as Curtis Bergen jogs toward us. Markus elbows me hard in the shoulder and I stand there rubbing it, wincing from the pain.

"Hey, Curtis," Markus says, standing aside so he can pass.

"Hey." Curtis looks at me sideways. It's not the first time Markus and I have had tension outside the change room. In fact, it's kind of a running joke. I know Curtis is going to go in and tell everyone we're out here at it again.

"Look, Nick," says Markus after Curtis is safely through the door, "just don't say anything, all right? Provincials are less than a week away–that's really all I'm thinking about. It's all the team needs to think about. So just don't talk about Philston Weiks. I haven't decided I'm not going. I haven't decided anything."

"But what's to decide?"

Markus just bursts through the door as if I haven't said anything at all. There's a *thwam* as it bounces off the inside wall and slams shut in my face. I can't wrap my head around what he's just said. How could he possibly not go? There's no reason for him not to! It's like he's trying to piss me off, like he can't give up being the great Markus Carver and let someone else do well for a change.

I storm in after my brother, and Steve Adders and Jay Bents are already on top of him. They're going on about last night's Leafs game. Markus is laughing and smiling, like he's just the same as he's always been. Like he isn't hiding anything. But that's exactly what he's doing. He's hiding something, a BIG something, from his team. And I'm the only one that knows it.

"Kev!" barks Steve Adders. I see Kevin on my right, already changed and dancing to the second run-through of "Rock Monster." "New song, man. Jesus!"

"It's tradition!" he says.

Everybody groans.

I drop my bag onto the bench beside him.

"Nick," he says, never stopping his groove, "where were you last night? You missed the draft."

"Oh, I guess I forgot." Kevin wanted to try doing an online hockey draft this year. We were supposed to make our picks last night. But after talking to Lindy, all I could think about was Markus and Philston Weiks. "Sorry."

"Nah, it's fine. You're just stuck with the autopicks and they are...pretty lame."

I shrug.

"Dirt," he says, scrunching up his nose. He holds up my sweat-stained kidney pads, nearly yellow now, and I snatch them back. "Hear of washing?"

I smirk. "Yours are worse, Kev. You just can't tell 'cause they're black." Kev's equipment always smells like soggy nachos.

He lifts up his jersey, showing off sweatless black pads. "Winter fresh, my friend. Like mountain mist." He turns back to the iPod dock, starting "Rock Monster" again as a shoe gets thrown at his head.

Markus sits across the room from us. He's already changed and tying his laces while Steve, Curtis and Jay yak at him all at once. I watch as Steve Adders elbows him with a grin. "Looks like she wants to get her hands all over your clock, eh? Eh?"

Lindy Hilner.

Jay and Curtis burst out laughing. Markus laughs too.

Dave Ingersoll does his best to join in. "It's about *time* you two got together."

Jay just shakes his head. "Brutal, Dave."

"Seriously though," says Steve Adders, "they've been hooking up for, like, a year now. It's kinda obvious."

Markus just shakes his head and keeps grinning. Like an idiot.

A year? Hooking up for a year? Why is he even laughing? Why does he laugh about everything, even when it's important?

"It's official now though." Steve pats Markus on the back. "Twenty bucks says she follows you to university when you graduate Maplehurst."

"*If* he graduates from Maplehurst."

The room falls quiet as every head turns to me. Markus frowns, and I'm glad. He's laughed too much today.

"What's up?" says Steve.

Markus's blue eyes are laser-focused on mine. I can practically hear him inside my head. He's daring me. I'm not scared.

"Markus might graduate a Philston Weiks kid. Isn't that right, Markus?"

There's a murmur of "huh?" and "what?" The entire team turns from me to my brother, waiting to hear what he has to say.

"It's not for sure," he says.

"They want you to play?" asks Jay.

Markus nods and gets up, turning his back on me. The team explodes into questions and congratulations, and Markus is swallowed up by everyone gathered around him.

"Really?" Kevin's standing beside me. "Markus? A Hurricane?"

"It's not for sure yet," I remind him. But I hope so.

That's when Coach throws open the door. "Game time, folks!"

Markus is the quickest to get moving, the rest of the Vikings following him to our game against the Timber Wolves. Just before he's out the door, Markus looks back at me. It's quick, but it's enough to see the disappointment on his face.

chapter six

Coach tells Kev he's taking the face-off as we file off the bench. I follow him onto the floor to warm up. I'm starting, again.

So's Markus.

Markus is taking shots on net with Steve, giving Chris Thompson, our goalie, a feel for the ball. Steve raises his stick, and he's pointing over by the penalty box. Markus turns and I watch him wave.

Sure enough, there's Lindy Hilner, sitting where she always sits, right there in the penalty box. The start of every game is the same. Lindy waves at Markus, Markus waves at Lindy. Lindy never waves at me.

But today's game is different. I try not to notice when Lindy blows Markus a kiss. *It's official now*. Markus doesn't even react, just goes back to tossing around the ball. Like he couldn't care less. Like it's no big deal.

I tighten my grip on my stick.

"Dude?" Kev hits me in the chest. "You all right, man?"

"Yeah."

He glances over at Lindy. She's smiling and bouncing in her seat as she watches my brother. Kevin turns back to me.

"What?" I say as he searches my face.

Kevin just shrugs. He knows exactly what, but he's not going to bug me about it. What's the point? He smacks my helmet. "Come on."

We haven't been warming up for long when the whistle blows. Kevin jogs to the face-off circle, and I set up behind him. Kev tends to pull straight back.

There's a hand on my shoulder, and I turn to see Markus. I can see his jaw through his mask, tight and clenched. He's pissed.

At me.

Whatever.

"This team loves the fast break," he tells me. "Head on a swivel, eh?"

"I heard Coach," I snap.

He smacks the back of my helmet, hard, and glares at me. "Shut up with that, Nick. You're the one who sold me out."

"I just told them the truth."

"That's how it is?"

"I don't see why it's such a secret."

"Nick!" barks Coach Preston. "Markus! Let's go!"

"Fine," grumbles Markus. "Be that way." And he leaves me to take his spot for the face-off.

Be what way? Right? He can't just go around smiling and lying to everyone. He can't act and talk like he's just one of us. He's a Hurricane. Maybe not yet, but he will be. He can try to make me feel bad all he wants. I feel fine.

Kev and number 15 on the Timber Wolves are down on the ground in the face-off circle. There's a blast from the ref's whistle, and in that moment, everything falls away.

No scholarship.

No Philston Weiks.

No Markus.

This is all there is.

Kev's faster than 15. He wrenches the ball back, directly at me. I'm knocked on my right side as a Timber Wolf slams into me, but I shove back and we fight over the loose ball. He's bigger, but he's clumsy. I manage to scoop the ball up and dangle around him. His jersey says 22. He's faster than I thought. Before I can look for someone to pass to, he's in my face, shoving me with his stick.

Behind him, I see Markus on the right, stick in the air, ready for me.

I check my time. I only have thirty seconds. The shot clock counts down–*28...27...26*.

Kev's on the left, dancing around some little squirt with *11* on his jersey.

Markus calls out, “Nick!”

21...20...19.

I look at Kev. He’s still trying to get around number 11.

Steve’s well covered, but Dave Ingersoll’s open. I growl against the pushing. Dave’s useless.

14...13...12.

“Nick!” Markus screams.

I fake left, and number 22’s out of the way, leaving me free to toss the ball to Kev.

He’s not ready for it, and he misses the pass. He and 11 scramble, both of them trying to get hold of the loose ball.

08...07...06.

And then Kev’s got it, but 11’s not happy about it.

05...04...03.

Kev takes a solid hit from 11 into the boards, and the buzzer sounds.

Damn it.

We’ve run out the shot clock. Timber Wolves’ ball.

Lindy resets the clock for the Wolves, but thirty seconds is more time than they need.

The next bit happens in a flash–number 11 passes off to 15, 15 to 22, and I'm on him, barreling toward our net, swatting at his stick. He's too big to care. I pump my legs as fast as they'll go. Just before I can get in front of him, he whips the ball at our net.

Bottom right.

Chris misses.

The score is 1-0 Timber Wolves.

My shoulders slump under the weight of my pads. Lindy's biting her lip–I can see it even from where I'm standing. She's looking at the scoreboard.

I'm shoved from behind, and I stumble, nearly knocked off my feet, as 22 laughs, pointing at the scoreboard. Twenty-two is Damien Sadowski. Damien is to the Timber Wolves what Markus is to the Vikings, except that Damien's game is a lot rougher. He's a real goon and knows how to get under a guy's skin–especially Markus's.

I turn away from Damien and check to see whether Lindy's watching. She already saw me screw up–she can't see me getting humiliated on top of it.

Kev's more mad about the push than I am.

"Hey!" he barks, stepping into Damien's face. Damien laughs and gives Kev a shove. Kev pushes back and then Markus is next to him, pressing his mask against Damien's.

"Feelin' tough, Sadowski?" Markus growls.

Damien answers him with a hard shove. Lindy's standing now, hands against the glass, wide eyes on my brother.

Always on my brother.

The ref finally breaks it up, and Markus runs up to me, grabbing my mask. "Stand up for yourself, Nick! What are you doing?"

I jerk my head back and he lets go, running back for the face-off.

Lindy watches him go.

Always watching.

I let the thick arena air fill my nose and lungs. My exhausted muscles feel like lead under my skin.

This is one game where all eyes are going to be on me. I'll make sure of it.

chapter seven

The whistle blows, and I try my best not to look at the scoreboard. I know what it says. Three to zip, Timber Wolves.

"Nick!" Coach calls. "Get over here!"

I drag my feet to the bench, eyes on the floor.

"Get in here," he snaps. "You either start passing the ball or the next time I call you, your ass is nailed to the bench for the rest of the game."

Great.

I plunk down next to Curtis. We're halfway through the third and haven't even gotten on the board. I take a long swig from my water bottle. I haven't even managed one goal. Not one. On the plus side, with me not setting Markus up the way he'd like, he hasn't managed to score either. Some superstar.

The whistle blows. Wolves' ball.

Markus runs toward the bench. Curtis gets up and takes his place on the floor while Markus stands in front of me, chugging back water. He spits some through his mask and frowns.

"Big man today, eh?" he says.

I take a swig from my water bottle.

He smacks me on the head and points to the scoreboard. "How's that working out for you?"

"I don't see you doing much to fix it," I grumble.

"What?"

I don't say anything.

"Whatever," says Markus, taking a seat beside me. "Friggin' baby."

We sit there in silence as our team struggles to repair some of the damage. And it's Kev who gets us on the board from twenty feet out.

Over the cheers, I hear Coach shout my name. "Get out there!"

I'm on my feet when Markus stops me. "You gonna share the ball this time?"

I ignore him and head out onto the floor. I share plenty. If I didn't share as much as I did, Markus wouldn't be getting scholarships to Philston Weiks.

"Yeah," Markus calls after me. "I'm sure Lindy's real impressed!"

A sudden pang shoots through me at the sound of her name. Her name out of Markus's mouth. Her name, related to me. I turn back, and he's glaring at me, Dave and Sean McDonald smirking beside him. My cheeks are red beneath the face mask, I can feel it.

"Nick." Kev nods to center, wanting me to take the face-off.

Lindy's watching from the penalty box, taking a picture with her phone. I feel sick.

She's been watching me fail all game. Everyone has.

And Markus knows.

He said it himself. *I'm sure Lindy's real impressed*. Does Lindy know? My eyes float through the stands, scattered pockets of parents, girlfriends, brothers and sisters. They're all chatting and laughing. Suddenly, I feel like it's all about me. Me and Lindy. The whole world knows.

There's a slam as Coach closes the bench door and Markus walks onto the floor. *Damn it, Markus.*

"Nick?" I turn, and Kev's looking at me. "You got this?"

I swallow hard and nod. Somehow, I've got to fix this. Somehow, I've got to claw my way back from the joke I've turned myself into.

Wolves number 15 is already in position in the face-off circle, and I join him, the two of us down on the ground. The whistle blows and I pull back with all my might, but he's got the same idea. He jams me up before I can get a good clamp on the ball, my stick locked against his. It takes all my strength, but I get a second when his pressure relaxes. I manage to scoop the ball left.

Steve's ready for it and passes it off to Kev.

"Kev!" I call. But he's not looking at me. He's looking at Markus.

Markus is locked in some weird dance with Damien Sadowski. Damien's all over him.

"Kev!" I shout.

He passes to Markus anyway. Markus steps around Damien and makes a break for the Wolves' net, with Damien wailing on his stick.

My feet pound the floor as I take off up the left side.

And then I hear it. Lindy's voice screaming over the shouts all around me.

"Go, Markus! Go, Markus!"

Go, Markus. It's all I hear, echoing off the walls, off the inside of my skull.

"Woo! Go, Markus!"

The air in my lungs is like fire. *Go, Markus. Go to Philston Weiks, Markus. Why won't you go, Markus?*

Before I even know what I'm doing, my feet slam the ground, driving me to where Damien is blocking Markus from taking his shot, and *THWAM*.

I cross-check him as hard as I can and he goes down, lying on his back on the floor, coughing and sputtering.

The whistle blows and the cheering stops.

There's silence for a moment, and then a quiet murmur in the crowd.

"Jesus," breathes Damien, standing beside me.

My heart pounds like it's going to burst through my chest. I'm standing over my brother, doubled over at my feet.

chapter eight

At night, my room takes on its own kind of darkness. It's a darkness that never really gets dark. Markus always leaves his computer monitor on so that it tints everything with a Smurf-like haze. It mixes with the neon orange of the streetlight outside our window and makes it look like my sheets are stained with prune juice.

I stare at my hand as I lie on my bed, inspecting the gross purplish-brown shade of my skin in this mixed lighting.

I've been lying here alone for over an hour now.

After what happened, Coach told me I was benched for the next three games. Provincials are next week. But after what I did, that's the least of my problems.

I roll over and grab my phone off my nightstand. Nine thirty PM. Markus still hasn't come home.

My head starts to itch, and I claw at my scalp.

The drive home with Mom was unbearable. "Have you completely lost your mind? He's your brother! You could have put him in the hospital!"

This was a bit overdramatic. Especially since he only sat out for, like, two minutes. He was on the floor again once he got his wind back. "What would you do a thing like that for, Nicholas?"

I kept my mouth shut. I knew why I did it. What's worse, I think Markus knew too.

The itch in my scalp won't go away, and I've got to use both hands to try to scratch it out.

I can't imagine what he's told Lindy. They're still out, the two of them eating sundaes at Freezo's Palace and talking about what a psycho I am. And maybe they're right. Maybe I am a psycho. Looking back, I didn't even realize what I was doing until it was done. It was like I had no control over it, like something took over my whole body.

Go, Markus.

I groan and squish my pillow onto my face.

I cross-checked my teammate. My own brother. I *am* a psycho. I can't blame them if they are laughing at me over ice cream.

Nine thirty-six PM.

I throw the covers over my head and shut my eyes, trying to focus on the sound of my breathing. I'm dreading Markus walking in the door. I can't face him. I just have to sleep.

I hear voices downstairs. Mom's high singsong voice, the rumble of Dad's and another deep talker as the front door slams shut. Markus. I can tell from the murmurs that it's a pretty chipper discussion.

How was your date? Did you try the Freezo Fudginator I was telling you about? Is she a nice girl? All of them opting to forget about the cross-check heard around the world. To forget about the bottle of crazy brewing upstairs. To forget about me.

The heavy thump of Markus's footsteps gets louder as he climbs the stairs to our room.

I roll over under the covers, facing the wall. Who knows what he's going to say? He didn't talk to me after I hit him. Didn't talk to me when the game was over, when we were back in the change room. Not one word. Saving it for the privacy of our bedroom, I figured. And here I am, hiding under the covers. Maybe he won't even say much. Maybe he'll just hit me, pound on me, while I lie here. Even up the score.

The door opens quietly, and I hear him shuffling around in the dark.

All my muscles go rigid, waiting for a blow from his fist.

Nothing.

He coughs.

The springs in his bed creak, and I peek over my shoulder. He's already got his head on the pillow. I guess the silent treatment is still on. I sit up on my elbow, staring at the back of his head. Part of me wishes he'd spring out of bed and just lay into me.

"What?" he says.

My voice catches in my throat–I'm surprised by the sound of his. "Uh, how'd it go?"

"Fine," he says. "We had a really *great* time."

I bite the inside of my cheek. He didn't punch me, but what he said was just as effective.

"Did she..." I stop, watching him slam his head into the pillow again and again, trying to get comfortable. "Did you...I mean, did you guys talk about what happened?"

"A bit."

I wait, hoping he'll go on. He doesn't.

"What'd you talk about?"

"She asked what the hell happened."

"Oh." I instantly feel sick thinking of all the ways Markus could have answered that.

He knows how I feel about her. He has to. *I'm sure Lindy's real impressed.* He said that. How could he have said that if he didn't know? "What did you say?"

He scoffs and slams his head into the pillow some more. "I told her you're color blind and couldn't tell whose jersey was whose."

No, he didn't. Or maybe he did, but still, she wouldn't have bought that. He sighs in the dark, and I decide not to ask him anything more. He doesn't want to talk to me. And whatever he told her, there's really nothing he could say that would make it okay.

"Benched?" he asks.

I nod.

"Are you benched?" he says louder, and I realize he can't see me.

"Yeah," I say. "Three games."

"You'll miss the first of the provincials."

I nod again.

"Worth it?"

I collapse on my pillow and sigh. We both know the answer to that. But there's nothing I can do to take it back now.

chapter nine

It's awkward sitting in the stands when you're used to the bench. For our game against the Wakeland Warriors, I got suited up and sat on the bench with the team. I figured there was a chance that Coach would decide I'd learned my lesson after two periods and let me out for the final. He didn't. I sat. They played. And Coach gave me another lecture about teamwork after the game.

This time, I chose not to suit up and to just sit with Mom.

It's ten minutes until game time in the first of the provincials, and everyone around us is craning their necks to get a look at me–Markus Carver's deranged, rabid brother. I'm already regretting my decision.

To my left I see Ryder Bergen. She's Curtis's younger sister and a year below me at school. She's staring at me sideways while she says something to her dad. Mr. Bergen sits up just enough to see me over Ryder's head and makes a sound like *puh* before he slouches back down. I wish Mom hadn't made me come today.

"Oh, I remember these boys," says Mom beside me, watching the teams warming up. "They're pretty good, aren't they?"

"The Hornets?" They're more than good. Last year, they nearly beat us in the final game of provincials. The game had been a struggle for both sides, but lucky for us, Curtis fired a laser at the top right corner in the last couple seconds of play. Coach Preston devoted a good portion of his lecture to stressing how tough I'd made it for my team by getting myself benched before we were about to play them again. I resisted pointing out that he had the power to fix that difficulty.

"They're good," I say.

"Hmm..." Mom pulls her mouth to one side, which usually means she's about to say something frustratingly parental. "Probably could have used you out there today, eh?"

Well, what am I supposed to say to that?

She makes a "hmm" sound again and nods to herself. Point made.

My throat feels dry.

"Oh, isn't that cute?" She laughs.

"What?"

"The timekeeper girl just blew your brother a kiss!" Mom's sitting up, straining to get a better look.

My eyes dart over to the penalty box. There she is, Lindy Hilner, at her post as timekeeper. It was bad enough to see her at the Warriors game. I'd caught her staring at me at the end of the first period. When my eyes met hers, she'd just pressed her lips together and looked away. Part of me was hoping they'd gotten someone else to keep time for provincials.

"She's Markus's girlfriend," I grumble. The words taste like iron in my mouth.

"I know." Mom smiles. "Lindy Hilner. That's her name, right?"

The dryness in my throat makes me cough.

"I need a drink," I say, hoping to escape to the food court.

"The game hasn't even started."

I slump down in my seat, the dryness beginning to strangle me. I don't know how long I can sit here watching Lindy watching Markus. Watching the Vikings fight the Hornets–without me.

The whistle blows and it's time for the first face-off of provincials. It's Markus who sets up to take it. It's Markus who takes possession of the ball. And in the first minute of play, it's Markus who scores for the Maplehurst Vikings.

Mom's on her feet clapping and cheering. "Way to go, Markus!"

Go, Markus.

"Mom," I shout over the buzzer. "The drink?"

"Wait till the period's over!"

I don't know if I can make it.

Markus's goal doesn't go unanswered, and it only takes the Hornets a couple minutes to get on the board and then some. I've forgotten just how good the Hornets are. Good and dirty. The crazy fakes these guys keep throwing at the Vikings are hard to get my head around, not to mention the laser-accurate passes. The only one who seems to be able to keep up is Markus.

Number 10, the smallest guy on the Hornets–though that's not saying much, as they all seem to be over six feet–fires a rocket at the left-hand corner and the buzzer sounds.

It's 3-1 Hornets.

"How old are these boys?" says Mom.

I shake my head. Even from up here, I can see that at least four of them have five o'clock shadows. If someone told me they were twenty-five, I'd believe it.

I wince as I watch Kev trying to shake one of the bigger guys who's hacking at him, slashing at his arms and torso. Maybe it's not so bad being up in the stands after all.

Another blast from the buzzer marks the end of the first period. Markus and one of the Hornets are yelling at each other, and Steve drags my brother away before the man-monster gets a chance to fight him. Lindy's nose is practically pressed up against the glass.

A five-dollar bill blocks Lindy out.

"For your drink," says Mom. "And I'd like a small coffee, please."

I snatch the bill, happy to escape, and pick my way through the stands. Passing in front of a pair of older ladies, I hear one of them croak out "Carver's brother." When I look at them, their wrinkly old frowns make my throat feel like it's closing up. I slam the rink doors open.

A man in an expensive-looking suit stands on the other side.

"Easy there, son!" he says. Three kids dressed just like him stand off to the side, laughing at me. I ignore them and jog toward the food court.

I've forgotten how crazy Maplehurst arena gets during tournaments. There are people everywhere. The lineup at Hank's Café is longer than I've ever seen it. That's all right. I'm not in any rush to get back to the game.

Behind me is Pad 2, and through the windows I can see the end of the Timber Wolves' game against the Dorland Devils. They're already shaking hands. I have to crouch to get a look at the scoreboard: 6–4 Timber Wolves. Good for them, I guess.

Coke and coffee in hand, I hurry back to Mom. She's standing in the aisle, laughing and chatting with someone. It's the same suit I nearly took out with the door earlier. The three kids who were laughing at me are there too, dressed like salesmen. Their blazers have a patch over the breast and immediately I recognize it—Philston Weiks.

"Here he is!" says Mom. "This is my son Nicholas. Nick, this is Mr. Trent."

"Nicholas," says Mr. Trent, extending his hand. I can see from his narrow eyes that he recognizes me from the door incident. "I've seen you play, son. You're quite an athlete yourself."

"Shouldn't you be on the floor?" asks a freckle-faced ginger with buggy eyes and a grin that looks more like a sneer.

I freeze with my mouth hanging open, too embarrassed to tell the truth, too scared to make up a lie.

"He hasn't been well for the last couple of days," says Mom, rushing to my rescue. "I told him to sit out."

My mom's a saint.

"That's too bad," says Mr. Trent. "Looks like they need you out there." He points to the scoreboard. It's still 3–1 Hornets. They sure do.

Mr. Trent and the kids nod goodbye and take their seats, close to the glass.

I look at Mom. "Are they here to watch Markus?"

She nods.

I hand her the coffee and swallow my rising cough. Philston Weiks is here, watching the game, and I'm sitting up here. Not that I want to go to Philston Weiks or anything. I just...I take a giant gulp of my Coke and let the bubbles burn their way down. I'd just like them to see what I can do.

chapter ten

By the start of the third period, things haven't gone much better for the Vikings. From the way he's slamming his stick against the boards, I can see it's getting to Markus. The score is now 6–4 Hornets. Markus managed another goal at the start of the second, but he's had no luck since. The Hornets are on him like he's the only Viking out there. Luckily, Kev and Steve managed a goal apiece, but the chances of getting ahead of the Hornets in the third are slim.

From my perch in the stands, I can see Lindy Hilner's lost about as much hope of winning as I have. She's chewing on her nails, her other arm wrapped tightly around herself, and she's shaking from the nervous jiggling of her leg. I've never noticed before how seriously she takes the game. I guess I'm usually too busy playing. I'm taking another swig of Coke when I realize it might just be because she and Markus are "official" now–his pain is her pain, or some Romeo and Juliet junk.

The whistle blows, calling my attention back to the game. Kev jumps on top of Curtis, celebrating another goal.

"One down!" says Mom, clapping.

And two more to go.

Markus doesn't acknowledge the celebration as he sets up for the next face-off, and I have to shake my head. He's too frustrated. When he plays like that, he gets sloppy. With two down from a win, we can't afford sloppy.

Markus wins the face-off and does his best to step around the bulldozer Hornet player who's on top of him. He takes a hard hit into the boards, and the Hornets take possession of the ball. No one's there to stop Markus's man-monster, but Chris manages to block his shot.

Markus comes off and Curtis takes his place. With Kev's help, Curtis manages to fire a rocket into the Hornet's net, tying the game.

My mom and I are on our feet. I can't believe Curtis did it! But Lindy's still seated, chewing on her nails, her leg shaking more than before.

"We might win this after all, eh?" says Mom.

"Don't jinx it," I say. From the look on Lindy's face, I'd say we were screwed.

The rest of the game is agonizing. The muscles in my thighs start to ache from sitting on the edge of my seat while the Vikings and the Hornets battle it out for the winning goal.

The time dwindles down, and before long there's only a minute left in the game. If the game stays tied, we're headed into overtime.

But Markus isn't having it. Like lightning, he intercepts a pass, snatching the Hornets' ball out of the air as though it was meant for him all along.

"Go, Markus!" shrieks Mom. I'm surprised by the fierceness in her voice.

Everyone's on their feet, screaming my brother's name as he steps around one Hornet goon, then another. I can feel myself screaming, my voice hoarse with orders even though I know he can't hear me in the chaos.

He fakes left and shakes the last man, leaving him free for the shot, and *THWAM!*

He underhands the ball into the bottom right corner.

"Yeah!" I scream, hugging my mom. An amazing shot!

"Attaboy, Markus! Woo!" She laughs, and everyone else is whistling and laughing all around me. And Lindy. She's on her feet, pounding on the glass and cheering, jumping up and down.

"Hang on, hang on!" shouts some man at the ref. "No goal!"

A man I don't recognize–from his grizzly-bear build I can tell he's a Hornet dad–is on his feet. He's pointing at the ref, shouting to get his attention. "She didn't reset the clock!" he barks. "It doesn't count!"

I look at Lindy. She's stopped jumping now and is answering the ref, who's pointing at the man in the stands. I glance up at the clock. It's still counting down, with thirteen seconds to the buzzer. In the frenzy, I can't say I was paying much attention to the clock, but thirteen seconds seems like too much leftover time.

"What's happening?" asks Mom.

"I think we might not get the goal," I tell her as we watch the ref and Lindy argue.

Markus and the guys are standing around, their arms out, heads swiveling from the clock to the ref. They look just as baffled as everyone in the stands.

The buzzer sounds as the shot clock finally runs out. The ref puts his arm in the air, shaking his head as Markus jumps around him, shouting and pleading. I'm glad for my mom's sake that we can't hear what he's saying. The ref points to the Hornets, and there's a cheer from their team as Markus's goal comes down off the board.

"What!" says Mom.

Curtis slams his stick on the ground, and everyone on our bench is shouting. I watch Lindy slink back into her seat, her face red from anger or embarrassment. We've lost the point. We're going into overtime. The ref's decision is final.

chapter eleven

We lost in overtime. The Hornets scored in the first three minutes and that was it. We lost. Out of the provincials after the first game. Losses happen, they're all part of it, and the Hornets were a good team. More than good. But Markus scored. We had the winning goal and then it was taken from us.

Because of the shot clock.

Because of Lindy Hilner.

"It's just kinda hard to believe, you know?" Kev hasn't been able to stop talking about it all day. He's facing backward in his chair, hovering over my geometry sheet. "I mean, she's been timekeeper for, like, what? A thousand years? And in the first game of provincials she forgets to reset the clock?"

I've been trying to block him out for twenty minutes, but he won't let it go.

"It sucks," I agree.

"No, that's not what I'm saying."

"What, Kev?" I snap. "What do you want me to say? Lindy messed up and we got screwed. Just have to try again next year. What can you do?"

"But she's been timekeeper forever!"

"So she made a mistake."

"Did she?" His eyebrow is raised, begging me to ask him to go on.

"What?"

"Mr. Carver"–Mr. Reid is looking at me over his glasses–"save the discussions for after class, please."

"Sorry, sir." I put my head down, determined to get at least some of this work done before the end of the period.

"*Did* she make a mistake?" says Kev.

"Turn around, would you?" I say. "You're going to get us thrown in the hall."

Mr. Reid clears his throat and Kev turns around. "I'm just saying," he whispers over his shoulder, "that it's weird."

I pretend he didn't say anything and force myself to do question seven. *Find the area of the quadrilateral in figure F.* Okay, so what if Lindy's been doing it forever? It's not like she's not a human being. Human beings make mistakes. I saw her in her car after the game. She was in the parking lot when we were coming out of the arena, and she was crying. She felt awful already. Kevin doesn't need to rub it in.

The bell rings and everyone jumps up, gathering their bags for fourth period, while Mr. Reid reminds us that the whole sheet is due Friday.

Kev slings his bag over his shoulder. "And it raises other questions, doesn't it?"

"What does?" We head down the hall, on our way to English.

"Lindy!"

"Just let it go, Kevin," I say with a sigh.

"No, really," he says. "How many times has she made this mistake before?"

"I can't remember this ever happening before."

"Me neither! But see, how can we *know* she didn't do it before? You know? I mean, if that guy in the stands hadn't caught the mistake at provincials, we never would have noticed! How many other times has this happened? It could have been dozens!"

"Be serious."

"I am being serious! Think about–"

Kev shuts his mouth when he sees I've stopped in front of a group of kids staring at the lockers outside the drama room. There are big, ugly black letters on locker 337–*BITCH* written on a slant in permanent marker. Locker 337 is Lindy's locker.

"Whoa," says Kev beside me. "Guess I'm not the only one."

"Only one who what?"

"Who thinks it wasn't a mistake."

Vera Stronnick and Tess Dooley are laughing and taking pictures with their phones. Two guys from ninth grade stand off to the side, talking about what happened at provincials.

"What, they think she didn't reset the clock on purpose?" I ask, a little surprised. Why would she do that? She made a mistake. A simple mistake.

Kevin nods. "Yeah. I mean, like I said, she's been timekeeper forever."

"Why would she do that?"

"It gave Markus time to get the goal, didn't it?"

I take a step back from him, shocked that he would even suggest something like this. "Who have you been talking to?" I say.

He moves in closer to me, lowering his voice. "The coach from Philston Weiks was there."

"So?"

"So he was there to watch Markus. Some of the guys were talking–"

"Which guys?" I say. "Ingersoll? Curtis?"

"Look," says Kevin, "if Lindy had reset the clock on time, there's no way Markus could have gotten that goal before the buzzer.

And imagine if the goal had stuck. How awesome would he have looked?"

I stare at the jagged black letters on Lindy's locker. I feel like I'm in the Twilight Zone. They think the golden boy fixed the game? That he used his girlfriend to help him cheat? Since when do people think anything bad about Markus?

I hear Vera gasp, and I look over to see Markus standing with his fists clenched and jaw set. His eyes are narrowed on Lindy's locker. I've never seen him look so angry.

"Guess the cat's out of the bag, huh, Carver?" says one of the grade nines with a smug grin on his face.

Markus's rage disappears for a second, his mouth open like he can't think of anything to say. He's confused, but I know now what the kid was getting at. How many people think the same way as Kevin?

Steve Adders is beside Markus now, a hand on his shoulder and trying to pull him away. "Come on, man," he says. "We're late anyway."

Markus follows, but not before punching the locker with a loud bang, making the niner jump. He may not have known what the kid meant, but if there's one thing I know about the rumor mill at Maplehurst, it's that word gets around fast. It won't be long before Markus knows *exactly* what that kid meant.

As for Lindy–I stare at the dent Markus made at the tip of the *T*–I haven't seen her at school all day.

chapter twelve

The rest of the day goes by in a haze. I don't see Markus again, or Lindy, but I can't get Kev's voice out of my mind. *And imagine if that goal had stuck. How awesome would he have looked?* Markus is an amazing player. He averages three points a game. A guy like that doesn't need to cheat!

As I walk up our driveway, I try not to think what I've been trying not to think all day. And then it's there in my mind and I can't help it. Is he amazing because he's been cheating all along? Like Kev said, Lindy's been timekeeper for two years now. I remember the way she bounced and smiled while she sang along to the radio that day she drove me home. *I do what I can*. That's what she'd said.

"Nicholas?" Mom's somewhere in the basement. It's amazing how she can know it's me from just the sound of my footsteps. "Your magazine came!"

On the front hall table is my and Markus's weekly *Sports Illustrated*, a Christmas present from our Auntie Charlie. I guess Markus isn't home yet, because it's still up for grabs. I pick it up and check out the cover–*Dormapov's return to the NFL*. I kick off my shoes and head upstairs, looking forward to reading the main article alone in the john.

I throw my bag on my bed and head down the hall, but when I fling open the door to the bathroom, I'm not prepared to find someone sitting on the floor.

"Whoa!" I fall into the towel rack, the surprise knocking me off-balance. Markus is sitting with his knees pulled up to his chest, his head leaning back against the tiled wall. "I didn't think you were home yet."

"Well, I am," he mumbles. "Do you mind?"

I do mind. He's not even using the toilet–he's just sitting on the floor. He rubs his shaved head and finally lets it drop to his knees, sighing.

"You okay?" I ask.

"Fine!" he snaps. "Can I get a minute here, please? This is the bathroom, isn't it?"

"So lock the door, then!" I shoot back. "How was I supposed to know?"

"Shut it, and I will."

I stand there awkwardly, shifting on my feet. "But I gotta go..."

He glares at me for the longest time, so I guess that's not enough of a reason to make him move. Finally, he goes back to sulking with his head on his knees, and I start feeling more uncomfortable with each passing second.

Carefully, I cross the threshold and plunk myself down on the toilet lid. "Is this about provincials?"

He looks up at me. "You heard what people are saying?"

I shrug. "Some stuff."

"Which stuff?"

I chew the inside of my cheek, not sure I want to tell him. He obviously knows already–why bother repeating it? "People talk. No big deal."

"Yeah." He laughs bitterly. "Easy for you to say."

We sit there silently, and I can't decide if I should ask him what's on my mind. It's probably just going to make him more upset.

"They think I cheated," Markus says before I have the chance. "Philston Weiks."

"Philston Weiks? What did they say?"

He rubs his face, covering his eyes. "They are rethinking my offer."

"The scholarship?"

He nods.

My neck feels cold. They're thinking of taking away his scholarship? Because of what everyone's been saying? No wonder he's sitting here like he just overfed his pet fish and had to give it the flush. The chill spreads out from my neck and down my arms to my fingertips. I'd been the one to tell the team about the scholarship. If Philston Weiks takes it back, will he have to tell everyone it's gone?

He rubs his head again. "They actually think I set this whole thing up with Lindy Hilner."

I nod, surprised at how quickly the rumor made its way to the Hurricanes. It's hard to believe they could take away his scholarship on nothing but a rumor. I watch him rubbing his head and sighing heavily through his nose. He looks so... defeated. "Did you?"

He looks at me. There's hurt in his eyes, and I instantly regret saying anything. "You think I would?" he asks.

I shrug and look down at the big ugly face of Dormapov on our *Sports Illustrated*. I don't know what I think.

Markus tears the magazine out of my hands. His eyes bore into mine, his cheeks puffing in and out like a bull's. I feel about as small as a dung beetle.

"You think I did this?" he asks again.

I try to find something reassuring to say, but I can't stop thinking about what Kevin said in Geometry. And it's not just Kevin, it's the entire team. How could they all think Markus cheated if there wasn't good reason to?

I guess I take too long to answer him. He chucks the magazine at my face and storms out, leaving me alone on the toilet. I smooth out the crinkled paper, and Dormapov looks up at me with disapproving eyes. I can't help but feel guilty. If Markus didn't do it, I just officially became the worst brother in the world. I sigh and quietly close the door.

Then again, he didn't say he didn't do it either.

I flip to page sixty-seven, "Dormapov's Return," and make myself comfortable.

There's only one other person who knows what really happened at provincials.

I'll have to talk to Lindy Hilner.

chapter thirteen

I don't see Lindy at school the next day. Her locker still has graffiti all over it, and the whole school's talking about what happened at provincials. Markus stayed home too. He said he felt sick. Mom didn't ask him the usual follow-up questions—*Headache? Or nausea? Do you have a fever?*—she just let him stay in bed. It probably wasn't the best idea, because people are taking Lindy's and Markus's absence as proof of guilt.

Kev's chewing loudly, stuffing his face with the plate of fries we're sharing. And by sharing, I mean Kev's stealing my lunch because he can't choke down any more of the soggy ham sandwich his dad made him.

"Think they'll bar Lindy from the arena?" Kev says through stuffed cheeks. "'Cause there's no real protocol for something like this. Obviously, they'll never let her be timekeeper again, but can they forbid someone from walking in the doors altogether?"

I let a deep breath escape through my nostrils. There's a group of grade-eleven girls on my right. They've been eavesdropping on the whole conversation. I just wish Kev would stop talking about it.

"What do you think Philston Weiks is gonna do?"

My stomach knots. "What do you mean?"

"They were there–they saw the whole thing," he says. "Think they'll be pissed?"

I shake my head like I have no idea, but I *do* have an idea. They are pissed. They are rethinking his scholarship because they're so pissed. I don't mention it though. I don't want to give Kev anything more to talk about.

"Kev!" We turn around to see Dave Ingersoll at the doors to the cafeteria. "Nick! Mr. Preston's looking for you guys."

Coach.

"What for?" I ask. At school, Coach Preston is just Mr. Preston, grade-ten Business Leadership. Lacrosse season's over, thanks to the provincials disaster.

Dave just shrugs. "Wants to see you in his room."

"Both of us?" asks Kev.

Dave nods, and Kev and I clear our lunch and hurry to Coach Preston's classroom. I feel that chill again, figuring this is about Markus and provincials. But what information could Coach Preston get from me and Kev? I wasn't even playing that day, and after listening to Kev go on and on about the whole thing, he obviously has no idea what actually happened. Just a lot of dumb theories. When we get there, the room's empty except for Coach Preston and Steve Adders, who is sitting on a desk.

"Hey, guys," says Coach Preston. "Have a seat."

We do, and Coach Preston crosses his arms, leaning his back against the chalkboard.

"First off," he says, "this is not about what happened at provincials."

My hands, which I didn't even realize I'd balled into fists, unclench and I take a deep breath, relieved.

"I don't want to talk about it, frankly," Coach Preston goes on, "and I don't want you guys out there talking about it either."

"He didn't do it," says Steve.

"No," agrees Mr. Preston. "I don't think he did. So until that gets sorted out, just don't talk about it. We don't need to add to the rumors."

I nod in agreement and see Kev shifting beside me.

"But that's not why I asked to see you guys. I got a call this morning from Coach Trent over at Philston Weiks."

I sit up straight, like someone just snapped my back with a wet towel. Philston Weiks?

"Coach Trent is head coach of the Hurricanes there, and he asked me to invite you three to their practice this week. Just to scrimmage."

The three of us are silent for a moment. I can't know what's going through the other guys' heads, but all I'm thinking about is Markus and his scholarship. Markus said they might take it away. And now what? They're already trying to replace him?

"But," says Steve, "we're Vikings."

Coach Preston holds up his hand to stop him. "Season's over. You're not anything right now. What you guys do is up to you."

"What about Markus?" says Steve. "Is he going too?"

Coach shrugs, but I already know the answer to that. "No," I say.

Everyone looks at me, and I swallow the spit clinging to the back of my tongue. "They are reconsidering his offer."

There's a bang as Steve hits the desk. Kev just stares at me, shocked that I didn't tell him sooner.

"So what is this?" says Steve. "They're just going to replace him before they even try to figure out what really happened?"

"What really happened?" asks Coach calmly.

"Ask Lindy Hilner!" he shouts.

"All right, that's enough of that," says Coach. "What did I say about adding to the rumors?"

"But this is crazy!"

The fries I ate are sitting like a ball of lead. This *is* crazy. I want to be proud, flattered, that they'd think of me, but I just feel sick. They said they were rethinking it, just rethinking. And now they call up his brother? For what? Have they already made up their mind? Are they already planning to replace him?

"Maybe so," says Coach. "But nevertheless, they've extended the invitation. Thursday at three thirty PM at the academy. If you want to go, go. If not, no skin off my back."

"We're not going," says Steve firmly.

"Whoa," says Kev. "I didn't say that."

Steve gives him an angry glare, but I'm not that surprised. Not with the way Kev's been talking all day. "Maybe we don't know for sure that he cheated," Kev says. "But we don't know for sure that he didn't either. I don't want to not go on the off chance that he didn't do it."

"He didn't!" growls Steve.

"Well, whatever," says Kev. "Like Coach said, it's just a scrimmage. I'll go."

"You're such a turdshit, Kevin."

"Hey!" warns Coach Preston, but Steve's already storming out, slamming the door behind him.

"What do you think, Nick?" asks Kev.

I lean back in my chair, the ball of lead creeping its way up my throat. I'd love to go. I want to show Philston Weiks I'm good enough. Show Markus. But this isn't how I want it. Not this way.

I shake my head. "I can't go. Markus is my brother."

"I'm sorry, Nick," says Coach.

Kev moves his chair closer to me. "Really, Nick? I mean, what if he really did cheat?

'Cause if he did, then there's nothing to feel bad about."

I shake my head again. "I don't think he did."

"Can you prove it?" he asks.

No. But Lindy Hilner can. I'm sure of it.

chapter fourteen

I don't mention Philston Weiks to Mom that night. The sick feeling I had at school still hasn't gone away, and it seems wrong to tell her while Markus is still moping around. He wore his pajamas while we ate Mom's goulash. Well, they ate. I kind of just picked.

After dinner, Dad's parked in his usual leather chair in front of the TV. Markus is sprawled out on the couch, so there's nowhere for me to sit but on the floor. We're watching the hockey game in silence. Markus hasn't said anything since yesterday.

His phone vibrates on the coffee table. That's the seventh time in half an hour.

"Holy jumpin'!" says Dad. "Popular man tonight."

Markus picks it up and turns the phone off.

"Not gonna answer it?" asks Dad.

Markus just shrugs and lies back down. No, he's not gonna answer it. And I know it's because Lindy Hilner is the one who's calling. Lindy Hilner. She's the only person I really want to talk to. The only person who really knows what happened. And what if she's not at school tomorrow?

Markus jingles the ice in his glass and sighs at the empty cup. "Do we have any more of that lemonade?"

"Check the basement," Dad tells him.

Markus cracks his back and gets up, dragging his feet as he heads to the basement like he's weighed down by a million tons of doom and gloom. I stare at his dead phone, thinking about Lindy, alone in her room, hoping for a response from my brother.

"Poor kid," says Dad.

"He told you?" I say, reaching for Markus's phone. I hit the power button and the screen glows white. That's when I remember it takes, like, two minutes to boot up. He'll be back any second. Maybe this was a bad idea.

"It's ridiculous," says Dad, eyes glued to the TV. "Once Philston Weiks realizes the truth, they're gonna feel pretty stupid about rethinking putting that kid on their team. To be honest, I'm not sure I want him playing for those people anyway, after this."

I nod, though I'm not really listening. I shake the phone in my hand, like that's somehow going to speed it up.

"Bunch of idiots," Dad goes on. "We'll see how sorry they are when all this provincials garbage blows over."

I glance up from the phone just long enough to make it look like I'm not up to anything. Dad's attention is on the game anyway. I look back at Markus's phone, still booting up. Piece of junk.

I hear Markus's feet coming up the stairs. The phone's finally on, and I check his text messages. There're about a hundred from "Linds."

"I need a pitcher," says Markus, and I quickly hide the phone in my lap. He's standing in the doorway, a can of lemonade in his hand. "Dad? A pitcher?"

"Check in the cupboard under the toaster," I tell him.

And then he's gone.

I look down at the phone in my lap and click on the latest message. **Please talk to me.**

"Ahem." I look up to see Dad staring at me. "I don't think that's yours," he says.

"Yes, it is." Dad hates technology. All phones and MP3 players and converters look the same to him. For all he knows, this could be my phone. He eyes me suspiciously, but he doesn't press the issue because, I can see, he's not sure.

I hear the cupboard door slam and know I'm running out of time. I don't really know what I want to do. I want to talk to Lindy, but how and when I haven't figured out. There's a clink of spoons as Markus finishes making his lemonade.

"Anybody want any?" he calls from the kitchen.

My voice cracks as I call, "No thanks!" I glance at the clock under the TV. Eight PM.

My fingers fly across the keypad. **Meet @ Freezo's @ 9—Nick.**

I stare at the message before I press Send. It looks kind of cold, and I remember what Kev told me about emoticons. I can hear Markus's footsteps heading toward the living room. I take a deep breath. Before pressing Send, I add one more thing.

:)

And then I put the phone back where Markus left it.

Markus lies back down on the couch with a big glass of lemonade, and I realize I haven't turned the phone back off. He places his lemonade beside the phone.

Please don't text back, Lindy. Please don't text back.

Slowly I reach toward the phone.

"What are you doing?" asks Markus.

"I just want to try a sip of your lemonade," I tell him, a little too quickly.

"I made a pitcher–just go get a glass."

"But," I say, "I don't even know if I like it. If I pour a whole glass and I don't like it, then that's a whole glass gone to waste."

"It's lemonade."

"I know, but you may not have used the right amount of water. Just let me try a sip, Markus. Jeez."

Markus rolls his eyes and looks back at the game. I reach for his glass with both hands, scooping up the phone along with the cup. I put his phone in my lap and hit the power button while I take a sip of lemonade. I glance down. The stupid phone needs a minute to shut down. I take another sip.

"I thought you just wanted to taste it," says Markus.

"It's good," I tell him.

"So get your own!" He snatches the lemonade and I lean forward, covering the phone that's powering down in my hand. He tilts his head and chugs, and I place the phone back on the table without him noticing.

I can feel the cold lemonade crashing into the hot waves of my nervous stomach juice. It's eight PM. On a school night, my curfew is nine. But tonight, curfew doesn't matter.

In one hour, I have a date with Lindy Hilner.

chapter fifteen

Sneaking out of my house at eight PM is pretty hard with a mother like Julie Carver. She spends all her after-dinner time in the laundry room, which is the only way to get to the garage. My bike's in the garage. I decide to walk.

Freezo's Palace is way up near the train station, so by the time I see its neon blue sign lighting up the night, it's almost nine PM. The walk wasn't so bad. It gave me plenty of time to think about what to say to Lindy.

But I realize, after working through a thousand different questions to ask her, that I haven't really figured out how to start this whole "is Markus a cheater?" conversation.

My palms are sweating like crazy. I'm about to get ice cream with Lindy Hilner. Is she going to expect me to buy hers? I'm the guy. I take out the change in my pocket and realize I only have six bucks.

I just won't have ice cream.

My feet stop on their own when I see her. She's sitting on top of a red painted picnic table, holding her forehead in her right hand. Her hair's in a tight ponytail, and she's wearing a zip-up hoodie. She's hunched into herself, shaking her knees. It's a bit of a surprise at first–Lindy's usually so bubbly and confident–and I check my watch, worried that I'm late and she's mad that I've kept her waiting.

Eight fifty-six PM.

No. It's not about me. I shake my head. *Idiot.*

"Nick?" She's spotted me, and she sits up straight as I get closer.

"Hey, Lindy," I say with a wave.

She keeps shaking her knees, the same way she does during a close game. I guess she's waiting for me to say something.

"Did you wanna grab a sundae? My dad's always raving about their Fudginator thing."

Lindy bites her lip, and her eyes look like two polished marbles, her usual black eyeliner gone, her lashes free of mascara clumps. She looks sad but still gorgeous. Her eyes well up with tears, and there's an ache in my chest. I want to apologize, make the flood in her eyes stop, but I know there's nothing I can say.

She shakes her head, and when she speaks I can hear the lump in her throat strangling her voice. "No, that's okay. You go ahead though."

She looks down at her shaking knees and hugs herself.

I don't really want ice cream either. I just want to talk to Lindy. I stand there awkwardly and listen to her sniffles before I sigh and take a seat beside her on the picnic table. The familiar scent of Trendy Femme wafts to my nose, and I take a deep breath.

"How are you doing?" I say.

She wipes at her eyes, still not looking up. "Not good. The messages I'm getting–you wouldn't believe how mean people can be. I'm afraid to turn on my computer. My house, it got egged the day after the whole disaster."

My hand jerks, instinctively wanting to move to Lindy's back to be reassuring, but my brain is quick to stop it. This is Lindy Hilner.

I mumble out the best condolence I can. "I'm sorry, Lindy."

"And now," she goes on, "Markus won't even talk to me! I've messaged him, like, a thousand times and he just refuses to respond." Her tear-drenched eyes meet mine. "Would you talk to him for me? Tell him I just want to talk for a minute."

I shift in my seat, suddenly feeling like I'm her best girlfriend or something. I nod. "Sure, I will."

"It's just"–she lets out a frustrated sigh– "this whole thing was the worst mistake."

"Mistake? You mean you–" I stop myself, afraid the question might make her cry more. Or, worse, make her mad at me. But this is why I'm here. To find out what happened. "So the shot clock. You didn't..."

Lindy looks up at me, scowling. "No, Nick, I didn't cheat, if that's what you're asking."

"So what happened?"

"I messed up," she says. "When I realized the mistake, I reset the clock right away, but the ref was right. I was too late. He wouldn't have got that goal if I'd reset it on time. But I swear, I didn't do it on purpose. It was a stupid, stupid mistake."

Relief spills over me, and I flex my fingers against the night air. She didn't do it. So Markus didn't do it. Lindy Hilner just proved it.

"Are they really taking away his scholarship?" she says quietly.

"They're 'reconsidering,' whatever that means."

"How did Philston Weiks hear about it so fast?" she says, slamming her palm on the table. "It was like they heard the rumor before I did!"

"Lindy," I say, "you've got to tell them. The Hurricanes' coach thinks Markus cheated. You have to go tell them he didn't."

She slaps her knees. "I tried! But even when Mr. Trent said he appreciated my coming to see him, I could tell he didn't believe what I said. I shouldn't have said anything about the Hurricane guy–it just made him angry. Said he wouldn't let me attack his players like that and asked me to leave."

"What? What Hurricane guy?"

She shrugs and wipes her nose. "This guy at provincials. He goes to Philston Weiks. He's a Hurricane. I went to get a tea before the third period and he was there. We started talking. He was saying stuff about Markus, about how Markus wasn't that great. That he didn't see what the big deal was, why his coach loved Markus so much. He sounded jealous."

The cocky smirk of the ginger kid is the first image that pops into my mind. "Did he have red hair?"

"Yes," she says. "I thought maybe he said something to Coach Trent after the game, that he wanted to make Markus look bad, you know? And I was just so mad that I kind of blurted it out. I asked Coach Trent if he believes every lie his players tell him, and that's when he asked me to leave."

My knuckles rap the picnic table while I think. "That's just stupid. Markus would be an asset. The Hurricanes should want him on the team."

"Should they?" says Lindy. "Markus is really good. He casts quite a shadow. You know what it's like."

She's looking at me sideways, and I feel heat on the back of my neck, remembering her face when I hit him. "I guess."

Lindy smiles apologetically, and I feel even worse.

"Anyway, sounded like the players at Philston Weiks don't want him at all."

"Is that what this guy said?"

She nods. "More or less."

The game at provincials was a good game, and Markus was practically carrying the team. If the Hurricanes are threatened by him, could they have lied to Coach Trent?

"Something's going on," I say out loud.

"What do you mean?"

Anger shoots through me as I picture that smug Philston Weiks kid fixing his blazer and talking to Lindy. "You think this guy said something to Coach Trent?"

Her brow knots. "Don't you?"

It's a good bet. Him or one of the other cronies who came to the game. "Do you know his name?"

"I never asked," she says.

The sound of my knuckles hitting the table gets louder, and I shake my hand to get rid of the pain. Markus could lose his scholarship. Lindy won't even come to school. All because some Philston Weiks Richie Rich decided he wanted to cause some trouble?

"Hey Nickadoo?" Lindy's resting her chin on her shoulder, and there's a faint smile on her lips. It's sad, but it's there. "Thank you. For talking to me and all. You're, like, the only person in Maplehurst who will right now."

There's a swell in my chest, and I try to hold back a smile. I'm proud I did it, made her smile. Even if it's only a little bit.

She nudges me with her elbow. "What are you thinking?"

I click my tongue. "I got invited to scrimmage with the Hurricanes on Thursday."

"What?"

I nod. "I told them no, 'cause of Markus and all."

Lindy scoffs, just as angry about it as Steve Adders was.

"I'm thinking," I say, rubbing the pain out of my knuckles, "that I should go after all."

"You think they'll tell you something?"

I shrug. "It's worth a shot."

chapter sixteen

When I tell Kevin I'll go to the Hurricanes' practice, he's pretty excited–until I tell him why.

"You're not gonna say anything, are you?" he asks.

We're standing at the gate to the Philston Weiks Academy. The driveway leads up to a big gray-stoned archway entrance and winds around to a second gate, like a horse-shoe. The lawn is bright green and well manicured, with an iron statue of a man holding a book in the center of it all.

"It's not that big for a high school," I say. From the archway entrance, the building extends to the left for a length of about two classrooms and to the right for about the same. It's two stories high. How many classrooms can there be in this place?

"What?" says Kev.

"I mean, don't get me wrong, it's a big mansion, but it's not that big for a high school."

"Dude," says Kevin, stopping me just as we pass the iron man holding a book, "you're not seriously gonna say anything to these guys about what Lindy said, are you?"

"Relax, Kev, I'm just here to play." I give him a reassuring pat on the shoulder, but Kev doesn't look convinced. Because I'm not really here to play. I'm here for Lindy. And for Markus. But how am I going to get anyone to tell me anything? I can't just walk in there and ask around. No, my best bet is just to observe. Keep my ears open.

Maybe someone will say something or do something that will help me.

Our footsteps echo in the front entrance and creak on the hardwood floor. The shine on it is blinding, like the whole thing's been painted with honey. I already feel defensive, as though I've crossed into enemy territory.

"Where do you think we go?" asks Kev.

Before I have a chance to guess, we hear footsteps and see a guy in his Philston Weiks uniform hurrying down the hall on our left. I feel my shoulders tense, wondering if he's the one who started the rumor about Lindy and Markus. He stops when he sees us. "You guys here for lacrosse?"

"Yeah," says Kev.

"Locker room's this way." He points behind him, farther down the hall, and the two of us follow. He doesn't look familiar, not one of the guys from the provincials. I let myself relax a little.

"Phil LeBlanc," says the kid, holding out his hand to Kev.

Kev grins, shaking Phil's hand a little too much. "Kevin."

Phil smiles and looks over at me.

"Nick," I say.

"Good to meet you guys. Coach says you're the best."

I can't help but stand a little straighter. I don't want to like the compliment, but I do. Phil leads us farther into Philston Weiks, and there's a flutter in my stomach as we walk. The school is a lot bigger inside than it looks outside. We pass by a stairwell and I smell that heavy chlorine stink. There's a pool downstairs.

We turn down another hallway, and here the walls are painted with swirling bursts of color. It doesn't take long to recognize that they're guys in uniform. Hockey players and figure skaters, streams of blue swirling around them like they're playing in a windstorm. And there are lacrosse players too. All of them wearing a silver *H* on their chests.

"You guys are in here," says Phil, stopping at a door marked *Change Room B.*

"So get changed, and I'll see you out there!"

Phil smiles and I nod a thank-you, but he's already hurrying down the hall to what I assume is Change Room A. Kev shoves open the heavy blue door, but I wait a second before I follow. Standing there waiting for Phil is the guy I saw at provincials–the one who talked to Lindy. He's watching me with a sideways grin, and when Phil jogs up he leans in and says something. Whatever he says, it makes Phil look back at me with a new kind of smile on his face. This one's not as nice as his "Welcome to Philston Weiks" smile. Phil tries to hide his laughter as he heads into the Hurricanes' change room. The ginger follows him inside, but not before giving me a wave. My heart starts pounding. That's the guy. I feel my molars grinding at the back of my jaw, and I push open the door to our change room.

The Hurricanes' *H* is enormous on the freshly painted wall, and I'm surprised to see two big guys–Hornets, by the look of their jerseys–sitting beneath it. They watch me with blank faces, fully dressed to play. I guess Coach Trent sent out an invitation to more teams than ours.

Kev's standing to the right of them, and I head over to where he's changing, throwing down my bag.

"Carver!" shouts a familiar voice. I whirl around to see Damien Sadowski. He's wriggling into his shoulder pads in the far corner, his mouth hanging open stupidly as if seeing me is the most exciting thing that's happened to him all year.

"What are you doing here, Sadowski?" I say. I'm a little embarrassed to see him here. Last time I saw him, he was standing beside me as we looked down at Markus sprawled out on the floor. Because of me.

"Got a call after your brother fixed provincials. What are *you* doing here? No loyalty in the Carver household, eh?"

I hang up my stick with a slam and fish out my Under Armor.

"Back off, Damien," says Kev.

"Hey," says Damien with a laugh, "good on you, Nick–really. Sure, that stunt you pulled at our game was a bit insane, but it was a long time coming."

I try my best to ignore him and take off my shirt, but he keeps going. "I know how it is. I have an older brother myself. And a sister!"

I raise an eyebrow at that, and Damien catches it. "Yeah, Donna's at Queen's for engineering, and Derek's at U of T for architecture. They got the brains, I guess. They'll be millionaires and I'll probably be sharpening skates at the Oak Ridge Pro Shop the rest of my life."

He goes quiet then, and his eyes kind of glaze over, as if he's seeing his whole skate-sharpening career flash before him. He looks so unhappy, I can't help feeling a bit sorry for him.

He blinks and snaps back to reality, shaking his head. "Anyway," he says, slapping his knees, "if Derek was good at the only thing I'm good at? Playing on my team?"

He laughs. "I'm surprised you didn't take Markus out sooner."

"What happened at our game," says Kev for me, "was an accident."

It wasn't. I'd hit Markus on purpose, and Damien had had a front-row seat to the action. I struggle with my shoelaces and glance at Damien long enough to see that Kev hasn't convinced him.

"Whatever," he says with another laugh, putting on his Timber Wolves jersey. "I'm just saying, I get why you did it."

I fumble with my other shoe, pretending I don't hear him, but I'm feeling a bit relieved by what he's said. It's nice to hear someone understanding instead of criticizing. Even if it is Damien Sadowski.

"Lucky break for you," says Damien, "him screwing up at provincials and all. Makes everyone forget what you did."

Everyone did forget, it seems. After all, I'm sitting here about to try out for the Hurricanes. I didn't even tell Markus I was invited, but I'm here, commiserating with

Markus's least favorite person. Really, I know I didn't deserve the invitation from Coach Trent at all. But I'm not here for Philston Weiks, I remind myself. I'm here for Markus. I'm here to prove he's innocent.

chapter seventeen

Kev and I step into the arena along with the two Hornets goons and Damien Sadowski, who's keeping close to me and Kev. The three of us are practically tied together as we come out of the change rooms. The doors open up under the stands just like in the NLL. The Philston Weiks arena is a little more intimidating than I'd guessed it would be. It's got one of those giant clocks floating over the rink, like in the pros. The Vikings' clock is just one of those crappy wall-mounted ones. If you come to watch a game at Maplehurst arena, you're sitting on concrete benches. And they line only one side of the glass. But here, the stands wrap around the entire arena. And they aren't cold, flat benches either. The stands here are made up of real seats, the kind that fold open, with armrests and everything. All shiny silver and blue to match the Hurricanes jersey.

Damien whistles beside me. "I could handle this."

The Hurricanes are already on the floor, tossing the ball around in pairs. But mostly they're just standing in little groups, yakking like it's cheerleading practice.

Coach Trent is sitting in one of the blue seats, typing on his phone when he sees us. He waves. "Kevin, glad you made it!" He stands up and walks over to us. He shakes Kev's hand, then holds his hand out to me. "Nicholas, nice to see you again." My chest swells with dislike for this man. For a second, all I can do is stare at him. He dumped my brother like he was nothing but a trading card, and now he's reaching out to me, waiting to snatch me up. I feel like a traitor. He probably shook Markus's hand too. He clears his throat and I snap out of it, shaking his hand as he tells us to join the others on the floor.

As we walk out there, I feel someone's eyes on me, and I turn to look. Phil and the redhead are standing over by the far net. They're smirking and laughing with a couple of their buddies as they stare in our direction.

My face starts twisting into a scowl. I take a deep breath and blow out through puffed cheeks. I can't get angry. Not right now. They think I'm here to play.

"Hey!" The redhead's stepped away from the group, looking at me while the rest of his friends snicker. "You're that other Carver kid, aren't you?"

My feet start to shift as the rest of the Hurricanes turn to stare at me.

"You're Markus Carver's brother," he says. "Am I right?"

I feel completely paralyzed by all the eyes looking in my direction. I could shake my head, deny it, but there's no point. Coach Trent knows exactly who I am. But I feel like when I nod, whatever cover I had in this enemy territory will be blown.

Kev steps in beside me, staring the ginger down while Damien stands up on my other side. That makes me feel a bit more confident.

"Yeah," I say. "I'm Nick."

"I remember," he says. His eyes are puffy, but I can tell he's not tired or anything–that's just how they are. He raises his eyebrows in a way that makes him look like Spock. "I saw you with your mom."

His buddies laugh, and I feel my insides wither.

"Saw your brother too–that goal of his."

I glare at him, daring him to say more. Lindy said the guy she talked to was a redhead, and I knew it even before she told me. This is the guy responsible.

Before I can stop myself, I throw it all out on the table. "Saw Lindy Hilner too, I hear."

He frowns. "Who?"

I don't bother repeating myself.

A whistle blast interrupts the conversation.

"Eric!" shouts Coach Trent, and the redhead perks up. *Eric*. "Bring it in," Coach says, walking onto the floor. "We've got some special guests with us today. Welcome Liam and Gabe, from the Westinborough Hornets A team, Damien, here from the Oak Ridge Timber Wolves A team, and Nick and Kevin, joining us from our very own Maplehurst Vikings. They're here to do some scrimmages with us, so thanks for being here, guys."

There's an awkward silence, and Damien fiddles obsessively with his jersey. Are they supposed to clap or something? No one does and Coach Trent moves on, but I'm not really listening. I'm studying all of the Hurricanes' faces. Most of them have forgotten I'm here and are focused on Trent's lecture. But Phil and that Eric kid aren't paying much attention and are mumbling to each other. I catch Eric stealing sideways glances at me.

Coach Trent blows his whistle. "All right, ten laps. Let's go!"

By the time practice is over, I'm so drenched it's like I did a cannonball into a pool of my own sweat. The Hurricanes work hard. They're not good by accident. As we head back to the change rooms, I get a bunch of pats and nudges from some of the Hurricanes, telling me "nice work" and "good game." Coach had put me, Kev and Damien on the same team with a couple other guys, and we were awesome. We really were. It was probably the hardest I've ever played, and it seemed like everyone noticed. No one has ever noticed before. Not with Markus around. But here, Markus isn't around.

Even Coach Trent looks impressed.

"Excellent work out there, Carver," he says, smacking me with his clipboard as I pass him. "Really great hustle."

"Thank you, sir," I say.

Kev's beside me, beaming as Phil congratulates him on a job well done, and I know I've got a similar grin on my face. I bite my lip. This isn't why I came. I came here for Markus. I shouldn't care about playing well, should I?

"I'd love to see you guys back here," says Coach Trent. "Same time next week?"

"Yes, sir!" Kev says for both of us.

Next week? Watch us play again? Could Coach Trent really be thinking of making me a Hurricane?

"Carver!"

I turn around, and Eric is jogging up to me. "Good work out there, man."

I don't say anything, remembering why I'm here. This isn't about playing for the Hurricanes. This is about Markus.

I glare at him, trying to find some proof on his face that he wanted to frame my brother, but all I really see are freckles.

He waits for me to say something. When I don't, he lowers his voice. "Look, do you have some sort of problem with me?"

"What makes you say that?"

"You've been giving me the stink eye all practice."

I chew the inside of my cheek. I hadn't realized I'd been doing that.

"I'm sorry I hassled you about your brother," he says.

"Are you? You seemed pretty happy about it to me."

He looks taken aback for a second, and I feel my temper getting the better of me. His brow knots. "Am I not getting something here?"

I'm suddenly furious, hating this guy for the cocky smirk that's constantly glued to his face. For singling me out before practice. For trying to be nice to me now. All I want is to get to the bottom of why he did what he did. "Did you talk to Lindy at the game?"

"What?"

I look behind me. Most of the Hurricanes have disappeared into the change room. "The timekeeper!" I snap. "Did you talk to her?"

His eyes drop, and he rests his stick across his soldiers. "Uh, heh, yeah, I did."

And then it's like my eyes go Terminator on me, and all I want to do is throw a punch in his big freckled face. I shove him with my stick, and he nearly loses his balance. "So you told her you hate my brother."

"What?"

"You didn't want him on the team. She told me everything. So, what? You and your buddies see a simple mistake on the clock and all your prayers are answered?"

"My prayers? What are you talking about?"

"You lied to Coach Trent! You told him Markus used his girlfriend to cheat for him."

"Whoa, what?! I did not!" He holds up his hands in surrender, but I shove him again. "Hey, relax! I talked to her, sure. I just wanted to ask her out. I didn't know she was dating your brother. But that's all I was doing–just trying to ask her out."

The idea of him hitting on Lindy makes me want to attack him, but I force myself to stay calm. "She told me what you said to her. She told me how none of you want Markus on the team."

He takes a step back, a baffled grin on his face. "What? What are you talking about? Look, she asked what we were doing there. I told her we were checking out our new guy. She got all giddy about him, so I tried to downplay how good he was. I tried to make myself look better 'cause she was hot, that's all! I never said anything to Coach!"

I try to make myself not believe what he's saying, but he actually seems sincere. I feel the hot blood rushing under my skin drain into my feet. If it wasn't him, who was it?

"One of your friends, then," I say. "Someone said something to Coach Trent."

"Coach Trent told us!" he says. "None of us thought anything of the time mistake until Coach brought it up at practice the next day."

I feel cold. How did Trent hear about the rumor so fast? Someone had to have told him. If Coach Trent told the Hurricanes, who told Coach Trent?

Eric takes a step closer to me. "We'd only benefit by having Markus on the team. What makes you think the rumor would start with us?"

Because it had to. If it started with the Vikings, that means it had to be–my pads feel heavy on my shoulders, threatening to pull me down–it had to be one of us.

"Nick!" Eric and I turn and see Kev at the change room, a wide, toothy smile plastered on his face. "Freezo's?"

The grin's so big. I don't think I've ever seen that many of Kev's teeth at one time. He's glowing.

"You know," he says, when I don't respond. "To celebrate?"

And then it's there, in my head. A terrible thought that his stupid grin won't let me unthink.

"Sure," I barely manage to squeak out.

Kev nods and disappears back inside the change room. *Celebrate.*

"Whatever happens," says Eric, calling me back from myself, "I hope Markus is here next year. I'd love to play next to someone that good."

I nod politely and start toward the change room.

"And you," he calls after me. I turn back, surprised. "It'd be cool to have you on the team too."

I don't know what to say. I've been such a jerk to this guy and he still wants to play with me. I smile and turn back toward the change room. Coach Trent wants me back next week. Eric would play beside me. I showed Philston Weiks what I can do.

But as quick as Eric put it there, my smile fades away. Someone lied to Coach Trent. And I'm worried that that *someone* wants to celebrate.

chapter eighteen

Kevin's nabbed a red-leather booth by the window when I walk into Freezo's. He's drumming on the side of the table as he reads the menu, full of energy and excitement. No surprise. Things have been going pretty well for Kevin.

"Nick!" He looks up from his menu and waves me over. I take a breath and blow it out from my cheeks. Everything he's said over the last couple of days is playing again and again in my head. How he's been talking nonstop about what happened at provincials.

But was Kev really capable of all this? Starting a rumor within the team is bad enough, and so unlike him. Could he really go so far as lying to Coach Trent?

"Dude," he says, huddled over his menu as I plunk down, "I think today's the day I go for it. Today is the day I try to finish Freezo's Monster Mud Mountain."

He's grinning from ear to ear. He's just so...happy. How could a guy with a guilty conscience be that happy?

He stares at me, and I realize I haven't said anything. "Uh," I begin, my voice cracking, "it's twenty-five dollars. That's a lot of money for ice cream."

Kev shrugs. "Yeah, but it's a special occasion. If I can't buy it now, then when can I?"

"What's the special occasion?"

"Come on," says Kev. "We're gonna be Hurricanes!"

"It was just one practice, Kev."

He rolls his eyes. "You heard Coach Trent. He invited us for next week! The guy was practically drooling on himself after scrimmage. We're in, Nick, I know it."

He bounces in his seat as he cranes his neck, looking for a server. My stomach starts to feel queasy. *You heard Coach Trent.* I did. He'd said great things after practice, and I'd felt...The acid in my gut makes a leap for my throat, burning the back of my tongue. I'd felt good.

"Hey there, boys," says Pearl, the owner, waddling up to our table. "What can I get you?"

Kev pumps his fist in the air. "I'm doing the mountain, baby!"

Pearl puts her hands on her hips, "That's a lot of ice cream, son."

"It sure is," Kev grins. "It's a special occasion."

That grin. That goofy grin gives me nothing but bad feelings. I don't want to believe Kev would do something so awful to Markus, but he won't stop smiling. There's this awful nagging at the back of my mind. Then I hear Coach Trent's voice in my head. *Kevin, glad you made it.*

Pearl sighs and writes down Kev's order. "All right. One mountain." She turns her head to me, and I barely register what she says. "I don't suppose you want one too?"

"Water, please," I say. My mind races. Coach Trent shook Kev's hand first. How did he know who Kev was? He only knew me because we met at provincials. He didn't say one word to Damien. Why was he so nice to Kev?

Pearl makes a note, takes my menu and waddles off.

"Nick! Water?" says Kev. "That's all you want?"

I nod dumbly, preoccupied with my thoughts. Kev keeps looking at me.

"I'll have some of your mountain," I say finally.

Kev sighs and sits back in his seat, drumming on the side of the table. The nagging in my stomach is throbbing, pulsing. Kev talked to Coach Trent. That's why he was so friendly. Coach Trent already knew Kev. But why? Did Kev want to be a Hurricane so bad that he sabotaged Markus?

"You seem happy," I say.

"Well, yeah!" Kev laughs. "We just made the best team around!"

"Since when do you think the Hurricanes are better than the Vikings?"

"Since always. You saw their school, their arena."

He had a point there. Everything the Hurricanes had was better. I'd just never realized Kev cared.

I shrug. "Yeah, well, when they find out Markus didn't do anything wrong, I guess we're back to grubby old Maplehurst."

"They won't find out," says Kev. I'm surprised at how quickly he says it.

"What makes you say that?"

Kev pulls a napkin out of the dispenser and starts to roll it up. "How could they?"

I watch as he huddles over the white napkin, rolling it as tightly as he can. "Do you think he did it?" I say carefully.

He looks up. "What's it matter?"

I lean in and lower my voice. "It matters because he's gonna lose his scholarship."

Kev rolls his eyes and sits back against the booth. I suddenly feel like I'm not looking at Kevin anymore. Like I'm looking at someone else.

"Lose his scholarship, lose his scholarship." Kev's tone is mocking. "What do you care? You hated that scholarship!"

"I did not!"

"Yes, you did," he says. "You hated that Philston Weiks wanted the great Markus Carver and not you. Well, you're very welcome, Nick! I got you what you wanted!"

His words feel like a cross-check into the boards, and my breath is suddenly gone. Everything that's happened, to Markus, to Lindy, is because of Kev.

Pearl's back with waters and cutlery, and the two of us instantly shut up. "Here you go, boys," she says. "Mountain'll be right out."

We both nod awkwardly. When she's gone, Kev leans across the table. "Philston Weiks doesn't want Markus anymore, they want you."

"Or you." I spit out the words.

"Or me!" says Kev. "But it could just as easily be you. So quit worrying about your stupid brother and start thinking about you."

Me. Playing for the Hurricanes. Traveling to the US. Getting scholarships to whatever university I want. And where will that leave Markus?

"I'm telling Coach Trent," I growl, getting up from the table.

"Go ahead." Kev laughs. "It's your word against mine. And guess what? You're the bad guy's brother. So good luck with that."

I stand there glaring at him and he stares back, completely confident. I'm not sure what to do. I remember what Lindy said, how Coach Trent dismissed what she told him. Who says he won't do the same thing to me?

"Whoops!" I'm bumped by Pearl, who's hauling Kev's bucket of ice cream onto the table. "Excuse me, darlin'!"

Neither of us acknowledges her or the ice-cream mountain, too busy staring down the other.

"You're not making that team," I say. He just laughs as I storm out of Freezo's. But I mean what I said. Kev will never be a Hurricane, because that scholarship belongs to Markus.

And I'm gonna prove it.

chapter nineteen

When I get home, I find Markus exactly where I left him. Sulking in our room. He's playing some shoot-'em-up video game that must have ten thousand levels, because he still hasn't beaten it.

"Are you talking to Lindy?"

Markus turns around and looks at me like I've just crawled out of a garbage can. "What happened to you?"

"A lot," I say. "You need to call Lindy."

"You're all sweaty," says Markus. "Where've you been?"

"Freezo's."

Markus raises an eyebrow. "Tough lifting the cone to your mouth?"

I wipe my hair out of my eyes and feel the sweat on my forehead. I try to catch my breath. I ran the whole way home. I see his phone sitting on his pillow and I grab it, throwing it at him.

"Call her!" I order as he snatches it out of the air.

"I'm not calling her."

"Markus, you have to. She didn't do what you think she did. She's just as innocent in all this as you are. I need to tell her what really happened!"

He shakes his head and puts the phone down beside him, turning back to his video game.

"We don't have time for this!" I say, and before I know it, I've slammed my foot into his chair.

That gets his attention.

"Nick! What the hell?"

"Markus," I say. "I talked to Lindy. She told me she didn't cheat. But someone told Coach Trent that *you* did. And I know who."

He's on his feet now, phone clutched in his fist, looking at me like I'm crazy. "Nick, what are you talking about?"

"It was Kev, okay? Kevin told Coach Trent that you cheated so that he could get on the Hurricanes."

"How do you know all this?"

"Because he told me!" I shout. "I was with him, at Philston Weiks! They invited us to one of their practices."

His brow creases now. "You actually went?"

"Yes, but only to find out what happened. Markus, Kevin is going to get to play for the Hurricanes. He's going to take your scholarship!"

Markus takes a step back from me and sits on the end of his bed. He bites his lip, trying to sort out what's just come flying out of my mouth. I don't blame him. I'm still trying to sort it out. I stand there, waiting and panting, with my hands on my knees. Finally, he looks up at me. "You're sure about this?"

I nod.

He looks away from me, but I can see his Adam's apple throb. He's pissed. And so am I.

He flips open his phone and starts typing. He presses Send and the two of us stand there, staring at his phone.

Seconds later, there's a beep.

"Lindy's coming over," he says and flips his phone closed. "What do you want to do?"

"We gotta stop Kevin."

"Maybe we should go to Philston Weiks, talk to Trent."

I shake my head. "Lindy tried that. That's not good enough. It's Kevin's word against ours. We need to prove it."

"How?"

I have no idea how. It's not like we can just convince him to fess up to Coach Trent.

It isn't long before Mom calls out to us from downstairs. "Markus? You have a visitor."

Our heads snap to the door and we sit there in silence, listening to the murmur of Mom's voice as she chatters away to Markus's visitor.

She's down there.

In our front hall.

Lindy Hilner.

Markus bites his lip and rubs his head. "What do I say to her?"

I snarl, annoyed that he doesn't know. "How 'bout 'sorry for being a dick'?"

He shoots me an angry glare, but it quickly breaks into a grin.

"Markus!" shouts Mom, and he's on his feet, giving me a slap on the back before he heads downstairs. I wait for a few seconds, listening to the thud of his feet on the staircase. When I know he's gone, I creep out of our room and to the banister and look down at the front hall.

There she is.

Lindy Hilner, standing in my house, talking to Markus. She's got her arms folded across her chest, and she's scratching her ankle with her other foot as she stares at the floor. She's mad at him.

Good. She should be.

Markus is talking to her, but I can't hear what he's saying–I can just make out the gestures. He places a hand on his chest. I guess he just said what I told him to say, because she finally looks up at him and nods. Then she smiles. That smile's all for him, and it hurts a bit to see it. She forgave him so easily, even after he was awful to her. He didn't even try to talk to her after the rumors started. Didn't even try to find out what happened. Not like me.

He motions toward the stairs and she starts to come up, so I dive back into our room. It doesn't matter what I did. Lindy likes Markus.

By the time the two of them make it to our room, they're already holding hands. I feel like I did the day I cross-checked him. But I swallow it back when Lindy flashes me that smile. "Hey, Nickadoo," she says. I grin as much as I can.

I tell them everything I found out at Philston Weiks. About what Eric said, and how nice Coach Trent was to Kev. When I tell Lindy that Kevin admitted to lying about Markus to the coach, her lips purse and her face goes red. I've never seen her angry before, and it's surprisingly scary. I wouldn't want to be the one to make her mad.

"We get him to confess," she says finally. I'm a little taken aback by the confidence in her voice.

"Confess to Trent? He never would," says Markus.

"So we record him somehow."

"Record him?" I look to Markus, who's just as confused.

Lindy nods. "We record him saying what he did, and then we show it to Trent. That's the proof."

"But how do we get him to say it?" I ask. "I didn't exactly leave him on good terms. He knows I'm out to expose him for what he did."

"Then I'll do it," she says.

I laugh. "You?!"

Her eyes flash, and I immediately regret it, wiping the smile off my face. "I mean, it's just, why would he admit it to you? You're one of the people he's trying to frame, remember?"

"He's got a point," says Markus.

We're silent for a while, trying to think up something better than Lindy's plan. I could maybe lie to Kev, tell him I've changed my mind. Tell him I want to play for Philston Weiks after all. But even Kev's not that stupid. He won't trust me the second I open my mouth. He knows me too well. I'm not evil enough. I'm not like him.

"Sadowski!" It's out of my mouth before I've even processed the idea.

Markus sits up. "What?"

"Sadowski! We'll get Sadowski to do it!" I practically laugh, imagining Kev talking to Damien about what he did.

"Nick," says Markus, "Sadowski's an asshole."

"Exactly!" I'm nearly shouting, I'm so excited. "Just like Kev!"

Lindy and Markus look skeptical.

"Think about it!" I say. "Kev thinks the same way as you, Markus, that Sadowski is a big jerk. What would Kev care if he spilled the beans to Sadowski?" I laugh again, remembering how Damien praised me for bodychecking Markus. Kev was there to hear it. "Kev'll probably figure Sadowski will congratulate him for it!"

"Won't he?" says Markus. "Sadowski hates me."

But I know that's not true. Damien's a tough guy, but he showed me who he really is at the Philston Weiks practice. "You're wrong about him. He'll do this. I know it."

chapter twenty

I take a long, deep breath, letting the flowers and cinnamon of Trendy Femme coat my lungs. Lindy is driving us to Oak Ridge. Markus thought it would better for him to stay at home, since he and Damien don't have the best history. Lindy had tried to convince him to come, but I'd agreed with him. We needed Damien and couldn't risk Markus and him getting into an argument and ruining the whole thing before we even had a chance to try.

I also hadn't minded the idea of a forty-minute drive alone with Lindy Hilner.

"What do you think the odds are he'll do it?" asks Lindy.

I shrug. "I don't really know." Damien's not exactly my friend. There's no reason for him to help me. But I saw a different side of him when we played together at Philston Weiks. I was so used to seeing him as the bad guy. As the enemy that needed to be defeated. But when I played with him against the Hurricanes, I got to see him as a teammate. He played with everything he had. Put it all on the line to help his team. He wasn't afraid to take a pounding, and he knew when to pass. He was selfless. A guy who plays like that can't be bad. Does that mean he'll help Markus? Maybe not. But I'm positive he'll hear me out at least.

Lindy turns her head to me. "So this could all be for nothing?"

I sigh and rest my head against the window. "It's the best option we've got."

We spend the next twenty minutes in silence. Lindy hasn't smiled since I broke the news about Kevin, and she hasn't even turned on the radio. It's just as well. I don't feel like listening to those bubblegum glitter beats.

We take the exit for downtown Oak Ridge and come to the arena. The sign for the Oak Ridge Pro Shop is written in big red letters above the arena doors.

"You sure he'll be here?" asks Lindy as she climbs out of the car.

I nod.

When we open the door to the pro shop, we're hit by the stink of gym socks and mold. There's one older guy behind the counter, inspecting a hot-pink mouth-guard like he's not sure what it's for.

I don't see Damien anywhere.

Lindy clears her throat, but the guy behind the counter doesn't notice. He hasn't so much as glanced at us since we walked in. I'm not sure he even knows we're here. She tries again, this time coughing, and he finally looks up, swiping a blond dreadlock out of his eyes.

"Need some help?" he asks.

"Yeah, we're looking for Damien Sadowski."

He blinks a couple of times, like he's waiting for me to say more.

"Uh, the skate sharpener?" I add.

"Aw, yeah!" He smiles. "Sharpee McSharpinson! He's at the back." He waves his hand toward the back of the shop, and I see there's a counter with a hand-painted Skate Sharpening sign. I smile at the guy and leave him to his mouthguard inspection. Lindy follows behind me.

There doesn't seem to be anyone behind the counter, but there's a half-eaten sandwich beside the service bell. Someone must be here.

"Ring it," says Lindy, nodding to the bell.

When I do, Damien Sadowski comes running from behind a bunch of storage boxes, cheeks stuffed with his lunch. "Hi! Can I–"

He stops when he sees me, and I have to smile at this other, unexpected side of Damien. He looks so professional in his pro-shop polo shirt and baseball hat.

I bite my lip as I realize he may not be happy to see me here. I'm bothering him at work. But that fear quickly goes when he smiles and holds up his hand for a high five.

"Carver!" he says, and I smack his hand as if we're old friends. "What brings you to Oak Ridge? We don't have a game that I don't know about, do we?"

"No." I laugh.

"So what's up?" His eyes move to Lindy, and then flutter back. "Need your skates sharpened?"

Lindy looks at me nervously, and I know there's no point in putting it off. Time to find out if this idea was worth the drive.

I lean my elbows on the counter and try to decide how to start this. "You got invited back to Philston Weiks, right?"

"Yeah," says Damien carefully. "Next week."

"Are you going?"

Damien's forehead crinkles. "Haven't decided. What's it to you?"

"Look, this is gonna sound kind of crazy, but I'm actually here–well, *we're* here,"

I say, waving Lindy into the conversation, "to ask you for a favor."

He already looks suspicious. His smile is gone and he's folded his arms across his chest. "Okay..."

"It's about my brother."

Damien sighs and unfolds his arms, shoving his hands into his pockets. He looks at the clock. Just the mention of Markus is enough to lose him. Good thing we left Markus at home.

"Look, I know you guys aren't BFFS or anything, but he didn't do what everyone's saying he did."

"And that's my problem because..."

"It's not," I admit. "But he doesn't deserve what's happening to him. He doesn't deserve to lose his scholarship. He was framed, Damien."

That gets his attention. His brow creases. "Who would do that?"

I nod and take a deep breath, hating that I have to say his name. "My buddy Kevin."

Damien's eyes go wide. He's shocked, and what's better, he's listening. "Kevin?

That smart-mouthed lanky kid you hang out with?"

I nod.

Damien smirks. "What a little shit."

I chew the inside of my cheek. Before all this, I probably would have punched Damien for saying something like that. Today, I have to agree with him.

"So you want to try and get his scholarship back?" He asks me.

No one says anything for a moment. I'm waiting for him to tell me to get lost. After all, if Damien helps Markus, his shot at going to Philston Weiks is gone.

"I know it's a big opportunity for you, Damien," I say. "But the scholarship *belongs* to Markus."

"I don't care about the scholarship."

His words hit me like a punch to the jaw, and I just stare at him.

Damien laughs. "Timber Wolves took provincials this year. Couple of college scouts from the States approached me about playing field lacrosse for them when I graduate."

I look at Lindy, who's biting her lip.

"You seem surprised," says Damien.

I don't mean to, because I'm not. Damien's an amazing player. I just didn't realize any one besides Philston Weiks had noticed him.

Damien laughs. "There're other places to play besides Philston Weiks. Too stuffy there anyway. Too many preppies for my taste."

"So..." I can hardly believe what I'm hearing. "Are you saying you'll help us?"

Damien sighs. "I've got a brother. If it were him, I'd be doing the same thing you're doing."

I look over at Lindy, who's already smiling.

Damien plops down in his chair and takes a huge bite of his sandwich. "So," he says through stuffed cheeks, "what do you need me for?"

chapter twenty-one

I'm alone in the Hurricanes' dressing room, changing the pocket on my stick. The strings look too tight, and I want to loosen them up before practice. I start picking at the knot, working on giving myself a deeper pocket.

I glance at the clock above the *H*. It's 3:55 PM. Practice starts at four, and I'm the only guy here. Both Kev and Damien are late. And the guys from the Hornets,

I guess, 'cause they're not here either. Did Coach Trent invite them back?

I wish Damien would hurry up. Lindy figured a phone would work best to record Kev talking. But both my and Markus's phones are a thousand years old and can only take pictures, no video. Damien's got a pretty sweet smartphone, so Lindy decided that was our best bet–if he ever shows up.

The door to the dressing room flies open and in walks Kevin. He stops, surprised when he sees me. Then he smirks and shakes his head.

My thumbnail stabs at the flesh on my forefinger as I struggle to pick the knot loose. A deeper pocket means you can do more moves and the ball won't come out on you. Makes your shot a little slower though. If the pocket's too deep, the ball will hit the top string as it's coming out and go really low. But too shallow makes it harder to hang on to and makes the shot go really high. I want that sweet spot, right in the middle. I've tried different pockets over the years, but somewhere on the deep side is what I like best.

I hear a snort and look up to see Kev, his chin in his chest, trying to hide his laughter. I feel my temper getting the better of me, my gut telling me to storm over there and punch that stupid grin off his face. But I don't. I focus on the strings.

Where is Damien? Did Coach invite him to a different practice? Why isn't he here yet? He said he'd be here.

I can feel Kev's eyes on me. When I look up, he's got his pads on already and he's watching me with a smug grin. I can't believe that just yesterday he was my best friend. What is he today? The answer to that makes me mad and sad at the same time. Today, Kev is the enemy.

I don't know if he sees it on my face or what, but his smile goes away and he rubs the back of his neck, clearing his throat awkwardly.

I reach into my bag and pull out some hairspray. I shake it up and start spraying the bottoms of my shoes. The floor here is kind of slick. Hairspray gives you better traction. Kev taught me that.

"Toss me some of that?" Kev's holding his hand out, wanting me to throw him the can. He's got his own. He's had a can of Bed Head in the side pocket of his bag as long as we've been playing together.

"Come on, Nick," says Kevin when I put the can back in my bag. "You're here, so I know you're not that torn up about what I did."

"I'm just making sure you don't make the team," I say.

"Bullshit," says Kev. "You want this just as bad as I do–that's why you're here."

My hands start to cramp up because my grip on my stick has become so tight. I can't deny that I want it. Not to him. He knows me better than anyone, and I've vented to him enough times about Markus and all the ways he pisses me off. I hate that I did that. I hate that Kev knows this about me.

"You're here to beat Markus," he says. But he's wrong. That's not why I'm here. I'm here *for* Markus. Not to beat him.

"You're here to prove you're better than him. Than everybody." He's wrong. Isn't he? I'm suddenly mad at myself for sitting here, trying to make the perfect pocket. Why did I do that? I'm not supposed to care. Not about Philston Weiks. I don't need Philston Weiks.

He's on his feet now, slowly walking toward me with a scowl on his face. "And when I beat you for the spot on the Hurricanes, you're gonna go back to being what you've always been"–my molars grind as my eyes lock on his–"a plug with a hard-on for his brother's girlfriend."

And I'm gone.

The rage shoots out of me like a bullet, and I leap at Kev, who falls back onto the floor. I grab him by the collar and haul him to his feet. He grabs hold of my arms, shoving against me. The two of us go flying into the wall.

"You're a loser," he grunts.

"Shut up!" I shout and slam his back against the wall as hard as I can.

He lets out a roar and pushes me back, the change-room door clocking me in the head as Damien Sadowski walks in on our brawl.

"Whoa!" shouts Damien, who's quick to pull me off Kev. He stands between the two of us, arms out to keep us both back. "What the hell?" he says.

Kev and I just stand there, panting and glaring at each other. All I want is another shot at his smug, lying face.

"What the hell are you guys doing?"

Kev wipes a bit of blood from his lip. "He started it."

My brain lights up with so much fury that I take a step toward him, but Damien shoves me back. He watches me with a knowing glare, and I take a deep breath. Damien's right. This isn't why I came here.

"Get out of here, Carver," Damien growls.

I grab my stick and helmet and slam the door behind me, but I don't head into the arena just yet. I stand just outside the door and listen.

"Crazy idiot," I hear Damien say inside the change room. "You all right, man?"

There's a grunt from Kev, which I assume means yes.

"Like his brother, eh?" says Damien. "They're both insane!"

This is a bit off Lindy's carefully written script, but I kind of threw our plan for a loop when I started a fight in the middle of the change room. Damien's improvising now. I wait for Kev to say something back, but all I hear is silence.

"I can't believe they even invited that kid here at all," Damien goes on, "after what his brother did. I mean, Philston Weiks is just asking for trouble."

Kev still doesn't respond, and my heart starts to pound. What if Damien can't get him to say it?

Damien's trying, anyway, plowing ahead in spite of Kev's silence. "I gotta hand it to Markus though. That stunt he tried to pull at provincials, the cheating and all? That was ballsy. I didn't think he was smart enough to come up with something like that."

"He's not," grumbles Kev.

"So why's everyone saying he did?" asks Damien.

"I guess someone lied to Trent."

My veins feel like ice, and I don't dare breathe in case I miss something. Damien's close. Kev hasn't admitted it–not really. *Keep going, Damien, keep going*. I only hope he's remembered to start recording.

Damien's voice is quieter. "Who would do that?"

The silence that follows is agonizing, stretching into forever. When I look behind me, I can see that the Hurricanes are already out on the floor. Eric's standing in the window of the door and waves at me to come in. I nod. We're running out of time.

Then finally Kev's voice is back. "You know the First Nations were the ones who played lacrosse first?"

My head jerks back to the door. What does this have to do with anything? Why is he changing the subject? I start feeling uncomfortably hot in my equipment. Damien's gotta get him back on topic.

"They played with, like, ten times as many guys as we do. Maybe a hundred times. For religion and things. Even to settle disputes sometimes. Their teams were practically armies," says Kev. "The games could last for days. Did you know that? The game made warriors. That was even what they called it. 'The little brother of war.'

Even through the door, I can hear something funny in his voice. Like he's not talking to Damien at all. Like he's just spewing whatever's in his head to no one in particular.

"What's that quote people say sometimes?" Kev says. "*All's fair in love and war*?"

I can barely hear Damien answer. "I guess."

"Well," says Kev, "let's just say I won the war."

"Nick?" I whirl around to see Eric standing at the doors to the arena. "You coming or what?"

"Uh, yeah, sorry," I say as quietly as I can. But it's too late, because Kev has flung open the door. It's so sudden, I nearly fall right into him.

"What are you doing, Nick?" He's frowning at me, and his face is turning red. I've never seen him blush. My eyes dart to Damien, and Kev doesn't miss it. His head snaps back in time to see Damien with his hand in his pocket. "What is this?"

Damien and I just look at each other dumbly, hoping the other will come up with something. But Kev doesn't wait for the excuse. He storms over to Damien and grabs the hand that's partway into his pocket. "What are you hiding?"

Damien pulls away and I hurry over to help him, but Kev is faster. He wrenches Damien's hand free of the pocket. His cell phone is in his palm, still recording. Kev's eyes flash, first terror and then back to rage. The three of us are frozen, Kev's hand gripping Damien's wrist, mine grabbing Kev's free arm.

Eric's voice breaks the standoff.

"Guys! What's the hold–" His voice trails off as he storms into the change room and sees the three of us practically pretzeled together. When I turn to look at him,

Kev grunts. Then there's a sound that makes my stomach drop into my heels. The phone hits the floor with a crash as its back flies off. It lands screen side down.

I scramble for the phone, but Kev's foot beats me to it, slamming down on it with a crunch.

"See you out there," says Kev. He storms past Eric, leaving me on the floor with the shattered pieces of Damien's phone.

chapter twenty-two

Damien bends down and scoops up his busted phone. His face is twisted like Kev has broken a part of his body. The back of the phone is halfway across the room. When he turns over what's left in his hand, the screen looks like a spiderweb, it's so badly cracked.

"Yo," says Eric. "Did that guy just break your phone?"

He knows the answer to that. He saw the whole thing happen. But why, he can't possibly imagine. So he just stares at us as we hover over the corpse. "Is it totally dead?" I say.

Damien runs his hand through his hair and hits the power button, but nothing happens.

"Dead," he says.

Dead. The phone is dead. And so are all my hopes of beating Kevin at the war he started.

"Let me look?" Eric walks up to us, the back plate of the phone in his hand. He tries to attach it after Damien hands the phone over, but it won't click into place. I feel like screaming. Like punching a hole right through the brick change-room wall. We're back to square one, and now Kev knows to be more careful. How am I gonna tell Markus?

"There it goes!" says Eric cheerfully.

Damien and I stare down at the phone, waiting to see whatever it is Eric sees. The screen stays dead.

"See?" Eric points to the little red light in the upper left corner.

"Great," says Damien. "The screen's dead. I can't do anything with it."

"Well, the SIM card should have all your contacts," he says.

"And video?" I ask, desperation soaking my words.

Eric shakes his head. "Naw, that's in the memory." He turns the phone over in his hand and points to the USB port. "Oh, wow, look at that. See here? The USB's pinched shut."

I can see that the plug is warped. I let out a frustrated roar and kick the bench behind me.

"Whoa, relax!" says Eric. "It's not the end of the world."

"Easy for you to say," I grumble.

Eric watches me sulk, a little surprised at how emotional I am. I can't say I blame him. "What's going on here?" he asks.

"Nick had an important video on there," says Damien.

Eric turns the phone over in his hands. "It's a Haywire?" he asks.

Damien nods. "Haywire 4."

"Graeme Henries has one," says Eric.

Good for Graeme Henries. I plop down on the bench and lean my head against the wall. I don't even want to go out there. There's no point. Or maybe there is. If I don't go out there, then Kev could be a Hurricane. Without that video, all that's left to do is make sure Trent doesn't pick him.

"I could try and fix it," says Eric.

I sit up. "How? It's completely shattered."

"It just needs a new screen, I'll bet."

"You can do that?"

Eric shrugs. "I can try. Come over after practice. I'll give it a shot."

chapter twenty-three

Eric's house is the biggest house I've ever been in. No, house is the wrong word. It's a mansion. Everything is new, and all the surfaces, from the floors to the counters, are made of shiny polished stone. They even have this bar-type room that they call a "butler's pantry." It's just there for drinks. Nothing else. Just a little room for drinks.

He brings us down to his basement, which is probably bigger than my whole house. The carpet is so white, I'm afraid my socks are gonna get it dirty. There's a big-screen TV sitting over a fireplace, mounted to the wall like a picture frame. I feel like I'm in a rap video.

"It's a pretty good sign, eh?" If Eric was talking, I didn't notice. I've been too busy taking in his palace of a house. "Nick?"

"What?" I say, nearly dropping the ice-cold can of Coke in my hands–the real stuff, not the no-name kind my mom buys.

"Trent inviting you back again. It's a good sign, eh?"

I flick the tab on the top of my can, not really wanting to say either way. Good sign of what? That they want me on the team? I don't know. Practice went pretty well for me, even though I didn't mean for it to. I was just trying to get in Kev's way every chance I got. For scrimmage, Coach split me, Kev and Damien up. I had to play against him instead of with him, which I was happy to do. I was so mad–about the phone, about everything–that I was on him like a bad stink. Coach seemed pretty pleased.

At the end of practice, he invited me to come back again.

I crack open my Coke and take a glug.

And I want to go back again.

I choke a bit on the bubbles, and when I'm done coughing, I say, "So, what can we do about this phone? Can you fix it?"

"We'll find out, I guess," says Eric, flicking on a light in a smaller room. A little office, it looks like, with gadgets and computers strewn across a desk. There are tools and lamps and little machines I don't recognize. "This is my dad's study," he says, taking a seat behind the desk and pulling out two phones, Damien's busted Haywire and Graeme Henries' pristine new phone that Eric managed to borrow. "Dad's kind of a techie guy. Loves tinkering with all these toys."

Damien crouches down beside him, and Eric flicks on the desk lamp. They look like two mad scientists about to do brain surgery. I lean in for a closer look. Eric turns over the busted phone, and all I can see is a mess of circuits that don't make any sense to me.

"What are you gonna do?" I ask, still not convinced the phone can be saved.

"I'm hoping," says Eric, "that if I can use Graeme's screen on Sadowski's phone, I can just use that to email the video to you."

He removes the battery and then, with what looks like a toothpick, picks at a teeny tiny yellowish square. With a quiet pop it lifts up. It's just a little flap of plastic, and beneath it is a silver slot. Then he turns to Graeme's phone and goes to work removing the screen.

"So," says Damien, "I'm still gonna need a new phone after this."

Eric smiles. "Well, if this works, then all you need to do is order a new screen. I can't give you Graeme's."

"How do you know how to do this stuff?" I ask, not convinced we won't break Graeme's phone.

"I don't know for sure," he says, and I wonder how much it will cost me to replace both Damien's and Graeme's phones. "I'm in here with my dad a lot. We've done a lot of fiddling with phones. They're all pretty similar."

On the back of Graeme's is the same yellow plastic square, and Eric pops it up easily.

"Cross your fingers, boys," he says.

He presses Graeme's yellow square into the busted phone and puts the battery back in. The whole setup looks like something out of a Bond film, and it doesn't take long for the screen to blaze to life.

"Ha!" Damien laughs. "That's my dog!"

On the screen is a black lab, smiling with his tongue out.

"You mean it worked?" I say, barely daring to believe it.

"Looks like it worked," says Eric. "Where's the video?"

A couple taps to the screen and the file's right there, waiting to be emailed to me. "Eric!" I blurt out. "You're a genius!"

Eric grins. "Happy to help."

But he has no idea how much he's helped. With a couple pieces of plastic, he's just saved Markus's scholarship.

chapter twenty-four

I'm sitting outside the Philston Weiks athletics department. I came straight from school and asked Coach Trent if we could talk. He told me to come back in an hour. He had a meeting, so I just decided to sit and wait. Too much has gone wrong in the last couple of days. I figured it was safest not to move around too much. Markus's scholarship could depend on it.

I study the giant trophy case in front of me. It's so big, it practically runs the length of the entire hall, an endless parade of golden statues and massive plaques.

My knee starts to shake, and I check the time on my phone. I've been sitting here for an hour and ten minutes. He should be here soon. My hands are soaked with my own sweat, and I wipe them on my knees. Soon Coach Trent will know what Kev did. I can't help but feel a little sad about what that means. Kev was my best friend. Once Coach Trent knows the truth, can Kev and I ever be friends again?

How different is he from me really? He was tired, just like me. Tired of going unnoticed, unrewarded. Kev's just as good a player as Markus. Was what he did that bad if I can understand why he did it? Understand having to deal with Markus's shadow day in, day out? I wince at the memory of Markus sprawled out at my feet after I hit him at our game. After all, I did kind of understand.

No. There's no excuse for what Kev's done. Coach Trent has to know. That scholarship belongs to Markus.

Just Markus and no one else.

I hear the jingling of keys and turn to see Coach Trent marching toward me. "Nick! Great to see you! Come in, come in!"

He unlocks the door and invites me to sit in a chair in front of his desk. The room is covered with just as many trophies as are in the case outside, and the walls have pictures of all the Philston Weiks teams. Some are so old, they're still black-and-white.

Coach Trent takes his seat and leans back in his chair with a smile. I know that once I start talking, that smile's going to fade away. My forehead feels hot.

"Coach Trent," I say, "I wanted to talk to you about something–"

"Me too, Nick," he says happily, cutting me off. "I was glad you wanted to see me because I have some exciting news. We want to ask you to come and play for us."

His announcement hits me like a lightning bolt to the head. My mind goes blank.

"What?"

He leans forward on his desk, grinning from ear to ear. "That's right. We still have the third tryout, but I've seen enough to make a decision. We want to offer you a place here next year. Is that something you'd want to do?"

At first, I can't remember why I'm here at all. Philston Weiks wants me to play for the Hurricanes? My insides feel like a washing machine. A thousand thoughts and worries and feelings, all tumbling together in a hot and cold mess. Have I played *that* well? I almost blush, not sure how to take being noticed like this.

Everyone has always noticed Markus. Never me.

They want me?

"Of course, you don't have to answer right now," says Coach Trent. "You'll probably want to go home, discuss it with your folks."

My folks. Mom and Dad. What would they say? Dad would lose his mind with pride. Mom might cry–she's emotional like that.

And Lindy.

For a moment I see myself in that blue uniform, the giant *H* on the front of my jersey. Lindy's sitting in one of those blue seats in the Philston Weiks arena, waving at me.

I sit on my hands and press my lips together. If I'm a Hurricane, everyone will see me differently.

"Nick?" says Coach Trent, looking at me like he's worried I'm going to throw up.

I might.

Coach Trent laughs. "You all right, son?"

I'm not sure. I came here for Markus, but Kev's voice is in my head. *Quit worrying about your stupid brother and start thinking about you*. I could. I could just shake Coach Trent's hand and thank him. I could go to Philston Weiks next year, go to parties in mansions like Eric's. I could be a Hurricane.

But if I do that, how different am I from Kev?

My eyes drop to my lap, and I start picking at my thumbnail. "Coach Trent," I say, nearly choking on my own voice, "there's something you need to see."

He sits back in his chair, and his brow furrows.

"Can I use your computer?"

Coach Trent hesitates, not sure what to make of my reaction to his invitation. He wheels himself back from the computer and I pull up my email. I click on the first one in my inbox.

MARKUS.

chapter twenty-five

My nose scrunches at the stink wafting out of my lacrosse bag. Sunbaked hot dogs and vanilla. I guess vanilla's the new odor-killing spray Mom's trying. It's no better than the lemons. The sun beats down on me as I sit by myself in the Maplehurst parking lot. The vanilla has started to smell more like burning socks.

I flip open my phone to check the time and there's a text. Damien.

Foos Friday?

I smirk. Next year Damien's going to Syracuse. He visited their campus this summer, and one of the dorms had a foosball table. Now it's all he ever wants to play.

Sure.

I check the time. Six fifteen. My ride's late.

The sound of heavy bass invades the parking lot until it's so loud I can feel it in my feet. Then I recognize the song. It's the theme to the new movie sequel *Frozen Heart*.

"Nickadoo!"

Lindy's Acura zips into the parking lot. She slams on the brakes.

"You're late!" I shout over the thumping bass.

"I love this song!" she says, ignoring me. She pops the trunk for me, and I shake my head while she grooves to the awful tune.

I toss my bag in the trunk and climb into the front seat. "I said you're late."

"I thought you'd want to shower before the game," she says. "I see I was wrong though–thanks for that."

I laugh. "What? I'm not that sweaty."

"I'm pretty sure Philston Weiks has some kind of stink monitor that you won't be able to pass."

"If that's the case, then you should probably take it easy on the Trendy Femme."

"Punk." She grins.

We fly down Devon Road at a speed that only Lindy would dare. She's a psycho driver. Since Markus started at Philston Weiks last year, she's taken on his driving duties, picking me up from practice. It's amazing what you learn about a person in the ten minutes you're trapped in a car together day after day. With Lindy, I've learned a few things: (1) Her taste in music is based only on what the *Fire Heart* movies tell her is cool. (2) She knows everything most girls are thinking, which makes her the best person to decode their confusing behavior. (3) She's crazy about my brother Markus, and they're perfect for each other.

"You guys gonna make provincials this year?" she asks.

I nod. "We're gonna destroy." This year's been a tough one for the Vikings.

Losing some of our best players before the season started was hard to recover from, but I'm proud of how we've come along. Coach Preston is sure we'll make the finals.

"Markus says he's going to every game."

"Good," I say. "He'll get to see what *real* lacrosse looks like."

"The Hurricanes play real lacrosse."

"They're all right." I shrug. "For rich kids."

Lindy barrels down Melvin Street and rockets into the Philston Weiks parking lot. I slink down in my seat as the people getting out of their cars give her dirty looks. She turns off the engine and sits back in her seat, looking at me.

"He's proud of you, Nickadoo," she says. "He tells me all the time."

I nod awkwardly. She's never gotten so serious on me before. Not since the drama of last year. I shift in my seat, feeling a bit uncomfortable.

"He wants you to take that scholarship, you know."

I do know. After I proved to Coach Trent that Markus was innocent, he met with my whole family to apologize formally and invite Markus to play for the Hurricanes. It was the least he could do, and Markus accepted. Then he offered me the same deal, and my parents went crazy, but I turned it down. Coach Trent tried again this year, but I still didn't change my mind.

It just didn't feel the way I wanted it to. The school, the team, all of it just reminded me of what happened with Kevin. I don't see him much since Coach kicked him off the Vikings. Occasionally we pass each other in the halls, but Kev never looks at me. Our friendship is over because of what he did. The lengths he went to just for the chance to be a Philston Weiks kid.

"Just think about it, okay?" says Lindy.

I smile. "Sure, I will."

But I won't. If there's one thing I can be sure of, it's that I'm a Viking. I want to be a Viking.

At the end of the day, the Hurricanes saw what I could do.

That's enough for me.

Acknowledgments

Thanks to Erin Thomas for pointing me in the right direction on this story, and to the fabulous ladies of the Sunday group (plus Sam), who listened before it was ready. Thanks to agent extraordinaire Ali McDonald, always ready for a pint, and to my fabulous editor, Amy Collins, who taught me a lot. Thanks to my parents for all their support and my brothers for the inspiration. Thanks to Ian, my lacrosse fountain of knowledge, always ready to talk me off the ledge.

And finally to Nick for lending me his name...'tis a good name.

M.J. McIsaac was born in Oakville, Ontario, and completed a master's degree in writing for children at the University of Winchester. She has three little brothers, all of whom play lacrosse. They inspired her to write this book. M.J. currently lives in Toronto, Ontario, where you can find her writing and taking care of one noisy beagle and a very hungry Lab.

orca sports

For more information on all the books in the Orca Sports series, please visit **www.orcabook.com**.